Praise for

The Valentines

What a great tale. Robert is one sexy mofo with an azz I'd like to pinch and a co—well, that's enough of my dirty mind...The plot is a good one. There are vampires, wolves and other beings, and the world-building is very cool...A great start to what I imagine is going to be a great series where everyone is intertwined. ~ *Miz Management*

Bravo, to the author, on what I though was a stellar performance with this story. I went into reading this story not knowing what to expect, and I finished feeling hyped for the next book in the series. I thought The Valentines: Robert is the start of a good foundation to a series. I appreciate and enjoyed the scenery, the action, along with the physical characteristics of vampires and werewolves that was created. Although this is a novella, the author still manages to incorporate a lot of information that explained everything so well. With talks of the council, humans, vampires, werewolves and mystical beings, this story does not disappoint.

I felt like we were almost given two stories, Robert and Sophie, along with William and Katie. William and Katie are both Robert and Sophie's brother and best friend. Although it felt like two stories, William and Katie's storyline within the book never overshadowed Robert and Sophie. Both of the main characters were intriguing the moment they met, bonded, reconnected and stayed together. Robert was definitely Alpha, he gave me shivers most of the time throughout the story and it doesn't hurt that his family is apart of the strongest and most powerful vampires. Sophie was inexperience's but did what she had to do with Robert to accomplish her gold. Of course, their physical chemistry was an added bonus.

Katie was the key with everything that is brewing between the vampires and werewolves and I can't wait to read more. *~ Romance Novel Junkies*

Total-E-Bound Publishing books by Sam Crescent:

Office Hours

THE VALENTINES
Volume One

Robert

William

SAM CRESCENT

The Valentines Volume One
ISBN # 978-1-78184-503-5
©Copyright Sam Crescent 2012
Cover Art by Posh Gosh ©Copyright 2012
Interior text design by Claire Siemaszkiewicz
Total-E-Bound Publishing

ROBERT

Dedication

I would like to dedicate this entire series to my sister, Emma. Not only has she supported me in my decision to write, she joins me in my long obsession with vampires. Emma, I love you very much and without your love and support The Valentines wouldn't have been written.

Prologue

The Council of Vampires, somewhere in Beyer West.

"You will allow this match to go through."

Robert Valentine glanced over at his father — head of the Valentine Corporation and leader of his family — feeling bewildered and angry.

"It is just another human family on the verge —"

"I don't care," his father yelled at him across the room.

Robert watched his mother flinch. His three brothers turned away, not wanting their father's wrath directed at them. Robert understood. These were perilous times and his father had no room in his life for arguments. His two sisters were not even allowed access to the Council's chambers. Instead, old traditions said they must remain outside at all times. One day, Robert wished to banish the old ways and start afresh. Rose and Dawn were equally affected by what happened in this place as he was.

Robert looked at his father. He respected him but there were times when he despised the way in which the man worked. The laws that governed their society were archaic. If they didn't change their ways soon, Robert believed it would get them all killed.

"What have they offered?" Robert asked, trying to take some interest in the situation, since it was likely to affect his future. At the moment he had no power to change the outcome of tonight's events.

His father nodded to the guards to open the connecting door leading out to the human visiting room. This allowed humans a place to sit and wait, and offered protection against the abuses of the outside world. Vampire protection, among the humans, was considered a last resort, and only the most degraded and those without pride accepted such an alliance.

A man and a woman entered the great hall. There was nothing fantastic about their appearance. They were dressed in business suits, neat and tidy, and he noted that they appeared to be in their late fifties. One of them carried a folder, which was odd. He assumed the folder contained information, but the Council usually had all the information it needed about human visitors petitioning for help. Beyer West might be a small town, but it was a Valentine-run town. His father was pedantic in his dealings with the human public. Every deal and alliance must be well-documented and sealed away for future reference.

"Mr and Mrs Ford, allow me to introduce my oldest son, Robert Valentine."

Robert acknowledged the couple, bowing, as was the protocol among his family. He kept his attention on the Council and his own family, though. He knew of the Fords from his own company dealings. They were a prosperous family who should have no need of the Valentines' services. Only last week Robert had checked the profit margins for the town's most affluent families. It all seemed rather odd to him.

The couple glanced nervously around them.

"We need the kind of protection you are notorious for offering," Mrs Ford said.

Robert noticed that Mr Ford was scratching his head and felt like doing the same. How could this company need their help? Last time he checked, Mrs Ford stayed at home with the children while her husband ran the company. Robert couldn't think of a single reason why they would be at the Council.

"We are not a security company, Mrs Ford."

"I'm aware of that, but we can meet the price that you have set." She handed over the file. "We've stumbled into some financial difficulty and we would also like assistance with this."

Robert Valentine opened the folder. An A4 picture of a beautiful young woman stared up at him, an innocent and carefree smile shining from deep within her.

"Pretty girl," he complimented her.

"That is Sophie. My only daughter and not a girl but a woman of twenty-one," Mr Ford corrected him.

"With all due respect, Mr Ford, I'm more than five hundred years old. To me, she is a child," Robert snapped, looking up to glare at the couple.

He couldn't deny the intrigue he felt about the girl, just from the picture he'd seen, but she was still a child. Her picture and family situation should not concern him or his family. Why did he suddenly have a bad vibe about the whole meeting? Robert glanced back at the file. The innocence clearly expressed in her beautiful features said that this girl hadn't yet been tainted by the real world. He felt a tug at his heart, knowing that within months the smile would be gone, replaced by a frown and wary features. That was just part of life, but something within him didn't want this girl to be affected by it.

This meeting was getting odder by the second.

Mr Ford retreated, leaving his wife to deal with the proceedings.

"The protection you offer is that no harm will come to the family, as well as you supplying money to cover our debts?" she asked.

His father nodded.

"The deal would be between Sophie and me," Robert interrupted. He found that he wished to see the real-life vision of the girl in the photo. To witness her innocence himself and to see her reaction to him. Would she be as affected by him as he was by her?

"Sophie is outside." Mrs Ford nodded at her husband to go and collect their daughter.

Five minutes later a small, plump blonde entered – or rather was pulled by the elbow into the room, one of their security guards holding her as her father walked in front.

"Get your hands off me," the girl snapped, trying to shrug off the guard's hold. After a few seconds of struggling, the guard left her at her parents' side. Her father reached out to take hold of the same elbow the guard had been holding.

Robert could see the fear on her delicate face. He could imagine that being in a room full of the most dangerous vampires in the world might be a little scary. After all, they could kill them all within seconds and no one would ever know what had happened to them. It upset him to see that the wary look he had predicted was already present in her eyes. Even now she held a world of knowledge that she had no business knowing.

The Valentine family was extremely powerful. No one questioned them. They were a family to be reckoned with. It must have taken guts to come here begging for help.

Sophie pulled out of her father's grip. She might be frightened but the little wild-cat had fire. He liked it. Robert felt the beginnings of a stirring in his groin. It would seem that his body liked her, too. He watched her, his eyes straying to every move she made, as she shifted away from her family to stand near him. She kept her eyes on the other creatures present. She knew the threat in the room, and it wasn't him or her parents—it was the mature vampire sitting further along the table.

Robert admired her for stepping closer, but also for being alert. Sophie Ford wasn't a stupid woman.

"My daughter will be the price for this protection." Mrs Ford gestured to her daughter, determination dripping from her tone.

Robert could see the mother shaking for the first time since he'd seen her. It wasn't an act...her daughter left her worried. Her daughter was unpredictable. Interesting.

"Does your daughter know what would be expected of her?" His father was intrigued by the family—Robert could hear it in his voice. Hell, he was intrigued, too—by the woman to whom, only moments ago, he'd referred as a child when speaking to her parents. The first human female to capture and hold his attention in a very long time.

He imagined it was the pure blonde locks. It had been so long since he'd seen natural, beautiful, long, blonde curls. Most of the women he'd met dyed their hair. The smell of the peroxide left a rancid taste in his mouth and the women always looked fake. He wondered if it was as silky as it appeared. The light on her hair gave the impression that the locks would be glorious and full. His fingers tingled to reach out and feel. He cut the impulse off. It wouldn't do him any good, having her running away from him. Especially when they were about to partake in an intimate binding ceremony.

"The daughter has a name." When she spoke at last, her voice echoed around the big hall.

He could hear her anger, resentment and defiance, all in that one brief sentence. His body responded to the outburst. All the blood in his body rushed to his dick. If he was alone, he'd take himself in hand and bring about a climax. It was like a beautiful pulse spreading inside his body, lighting up his world and mind. He would willingly have her talk the whole night away. In fact, he would fuck his fist as she whispered sexy, slutty stories to him. Robert shook his head. The woman stood less than three feet away — having sexy thoughts wouldn't get him in her good books. First, he needed to make sure she agreed to the connection. At least he could say that her voice was pleasing to his ears, even edged with anger.

"Well, then, be kind enough to share it with us," Robert Valentine senior offered. Robert could tell that his father was amused by the girl's guts. Very few humans had as much spirit when faced with something so much stronger than them.

"Sophie."

"Well, does Sophie—"

"Sophie is the one you should be talking to." Sophie unfolded her arms. She passed her parents, sending them a glare that clearly told them to back off. She moved closer to the centre stage, next to Robert.

Now he could smell her heavenly fragrance. Even her scent was delightful. He could live with this girl. Robert didn't doubt it. The good thing about being a vampire was the ability to know and make up one's mind when faced with something like this. It was why they were stronger. They took risks. This woman, he knew in his soul—the little he had, if he even had one at all—was meant for him. He had been taken by her at once, and he wanted her.

He admired her spunk, her beauty and her tantalising voice. "Excuse me, Miss, but you must deal with respect—"

"With all due respect, sir, I give my respect only to people who have earned it. And since, by definition, a person is someone who breathes, you don't qualify."

Gasps of outrage filled the room. If Robert hadn't been so amused by this little feminine package, he might have gathered the energy to be insulted.

"I could have you killed."

"You can try—but just like you, I have a lot of backing. Besides, last I heard the humans were looking for any excuse to kick your sorry asses out of this town for good."

Murmurs of curiosity replaced the outrage. She had them intrigued. Shit, she had *him* intrigued—but for an entirely different reason. He imagined the whole Council weren't visualising her naked and spread out on their silk sheets driving their cocks into her wet heat. When he took her she would be slick and melting—he'd make sure of it with his tongue.

"Care to tell us of whom or what you speak?"

"Nope."

Silence descended on the hall. For the first time in centuries, a human was in control of the proceedings...and the vampires didn't like it.

"My daughter can be a little headstrong—"

"Mrs Ford, your daughter is handling herself perfectly," one of the Council members interrupted her.

So, her attitude was impressing more than just him. It was good to know. It suggested that they were going to agree to this bond. Sophie was either stupid, or indeed had knowledge the Council would want.

He was pleased. She had impressed him, and not taking her as a bond mate would be a huge mistake. She was strong and brave—a perfect combination for a vampire to mate with.

Robert was looking forward to it.

"My parents have bargained me away as the price for protection. I believe it is only fair that I get to make the negotiations," Sophie said to the room at large.

"What if we only wish to deal with your parents?" Robert asked her. He wanted her undivided attention focused purely on him. To have those eyes staring into his own.

She turned her interest to him, fire flaring from the bluest eyes he'd ever seen. Having those eyes on him was worth her fury.

That's it, my little hell-cat—burn me with your eyes.

"Then no deal. They don't get their protection and you don't get me." She turned to the rest of the room. "I know the procedure—the blood bond that my parents want to happen requires a willing sacrifice."

"What about the 'virgin' part?" Robert was having fun. This woman was a complete contrast to every other human female he'd ever come into contact with. He saw her blush and knew her innocence was intact. His body reacted violently to the knowledge that he would be the first and the last man to enter her body. His mind filled with images of taking her. How he would get her nice and wet, teasing her wet pussy until she was begging for his touch. Robert couldn't stop his mind reacting. For the first time he needed a woman, and not just any woman, but Sophie Ford. His cock tented his trousers — if he was a human male he'd be embarrassed. He wanted the ceremony done and this woman naked beneath him as he drove his dick inside her. Vulgar words, but necessary. This virgin would be his. He would make certain of it.

"I've got that part as well."

She shocked the whole hall of vampires when she pulled out a tiny pocket knife. She should have been searched before she was allowed onto the premises. No weapons were permitted in the building. The soldiers tensed and went for the guns at their sides. Bullets intended to kill any non-vampire species. Robert waited, knowing Sophie had no intention to harm. She wanted this deal as much as any of them, he was sure of it.

Sophie slit a tiny cut on the tender flesh inside her wrist. She turned her wrist up, displaying it to the others before moving to him for inspection.

The smell of blood permeated the room. The scent reminded Robert of vanilla and honey. He took hold of her wrist. He could feel the rapid beat of her pulse, giving away how scared she actually was. Sophie might talk tough but the little cat didn't play it rough. He smiled at her, trying to calm her erratic nerves.

He flicked his tongue out, swiping the offered cut. The saliva his body created sealed the wound at once. Just a drop and he could taste her world on his tongue. She was indeed a virgin. Her blood tasted of the innocence of her body, the tender, caring nature of her soul...and the pain in her heart. Not every person's blood was the same. The flavour differed for every person. If a whore had presented her wrist, her essence would have been dirty and soiled, like the world around her, on his lips. However, if a woman who'd been a whore cleaned up her act and stopped sleeping with men for money as she had in the past, then her blood would become clean—but not pure. There was a difference between clean blood and pure blood. Sophie's blood would go for thousands of pounds on the black market.

He experienced the flavour of her emotions on his tongue. Her fear of her predicament but her very nature stopped her from losing control and giving in to her enemies… and she considered her parents the enemy. She wasn't fighting for them, but for herself and her friend.

If only humans knew how much information they were giving away just through a drop of blood.

"She matches the terms of the contract," Robert said, still holding her wrist in his grip.

Sophie wanted protection and he would make sure she got it.

"I want to add to the contract. My parents only negotiated for themselves—their wealth and protection guaranteed."

"State your desires."

"I want the deal to be extended to *my* loved ones. The people in my heart, whom I care about." Sophie pressed a hand to her heart.

"We can't do that," Robert's father told her.

"Yes, you can. Through the blood bond, the vampire to whom I become bound will have complete access to my thoughts, my essence, my very soul. In other words, he will have everything that is me. By that, I mean that I'll be owned by him and him alone. Through that connection, he can create a link that will stop any harm coming to my friends — to my loved ones."

Robert watched her. She was hiding something, he was sure of it. She wasn't worried about her siblings — she was worried about one particular friend. A female friend.

"That is *if* a lifelong blood bond is brought into effect," his father said.

"I'm prepared to do it."

"Do you know what you'll be agreeing to?" Robert asked.

Sophie nodded but didn't speak.

"You'd be my woman, completely, to suck and fuck as I desired."

"Robert, stop being crude," his father said.

"By the blood bond she has a right to know."

"And by that very bond I agree to the terms set out before me. I might be a woman but I know my own mind," Sophie interrupted.

His father was not a stupid man. He was hard and blunt, but not stupid. A connection like this could strengthen his family. He would be able to sense great power — power that the Fords must have access to. Otherwise, their enquiry would have been pushed aside. Blood bonds like this, between a human family and an immortal, were few and far between.

For the most part, humans were there for blood — nothing more. Maybe the occasional screw.

Robert wished he could see inside her head and know what she was holding back from them.

"You will come willingly?"

The most important element of the blood bond ceremony was that the human taking part must be agreeable. The bond would not work without it — the mind and the body had to be in sync.

"Provided my terms are met."

His father sat back, looking at Sophie with his head cocked to one side.

A tiny little blonde — plump and delicious — full of attitude. She was hiding something. Robert could sense it, even if the others could not. Yet this girl was strong. Her destiny was as a bond mate.

"The full ceremony will begin this evening. Take Miss Ford up to her chambers and have the ceremony room prepared and ready. I want this done immediately. Mr and Mrs Ford, your presence will be necessary for tonight only."

With a shove of his hand, he dismissed the humans. Robert watched as Sophie was led out by a female blood donor they kept on tap for whenever sustenance was needed. His mother followed close behind them. He knew they would collect his two sisters before they began making preparations.

Sophie turned back once to look at him.

He noticed the curiosity in her eyes. He had suddenly found a human female worthy of his attention and admiration. Robert smiled at her, watching as she blushed.

Once all the women had gone, the real problems started for the Council, a select group of people who took the care of the vampire world seriously.

"We already have too much at stake, what with all the bloody vampire hunters."

The Council members nodded their heads in agreement. All of them were prepared to agree to anything Robert Valentine Senior offered. His father was not only the most powerful among them, but, over the centuries, he'd been responsible for keeping relative peace between the vampires and the other species. He had gained respect through listening and taking his time to make a decision. Robert Senior fought battles with his head.

"We need more protection in place."

"The wolves are responsible."

"The wolves wouldn't dare."

"How can we know for sure?"

The Council meeting went on and on. The fight about the wolves would continue for decades. Robert was more interested in the little blonde whom, in just a few hours, he would be bound to protect for the rest of their lives. He was looking forward to it.

Several hours later, Sophie was shaking inside. Her long, silky blonde hair, brushed into a glowing mass, rested around her like a cape. She wore a white gown so sheer that she thought everyone present at the ceremony would be able to see her naked body underneath. Sophie had tried to argue with the vampire women, who'd prepared her without speaking a word to her. She had wanted to wear at least her underwear, but they had got rid of all of her clothes. Her face was washed and clean of make-up. Neither of the women spoke to her—instead she was treated more as an object than a person.

She'd been told to wait for them to escort her down to the main ceremonial chamber. Her hands wouldn't stop shaking.

Sophie wondered if she was doing the right thing. She shook her head. She didn't have a choice. She needed to do this. Her friend would be protected. She loved her brothers, but they could guard themselves. And her parents had shown that they were more than capable of looking out for themselves, whatever the price. She would save them all through this bond, but Katie was the one who deserved it—who needed it.

Once she was under the care of a blood bond, no one could get to her. She would be safe, even from the vampires.

Sophie released a sigh of relief. After spending weeks planning for this, it seemed surreal that it was finally happening.

She hoped she would have time to bask in the happiness she was feeling. It was as though a huge weight had been removed from her shoulders.

The door to her room opened and the mother of the vampire she was about to be bonded to came in. Her smile was happy and cheery.

"Are you ready?"

Everything she had heard about vampires — all the rumours — had prepared Sophie for the prospect of dealing with evil creatures of the night. This woman turned her ideas upside down. They might not have spoken a word, but the gentle way the woman prepared her and the kindness Sophie could see reflecting from her eyes told her so much about the older woman. This woman — or vampire — wasn't evil.

Sophie nodded. The woman extended her hand, but Sophie refused to take it and followed close behind her instead. She couldn't take in her surroundings. She couldn't hear anything over her heartbeat. Every step felt like the tick of a great clock, marking away the remaining seconds of her life.

Sophie, aged twenty-one, was about to enter into a lifelong contract.

She wouldn't break down. She needed to do this. She closed her eyes and pictured Katie. Her best friend. She was doing this for her.

She entered the chamber through a heavy wooden door. Sophie believed she could sense all the other men and women who had faced the end of their lives in this very room. Those who had sold themselves for the protection of others. Her parents were on one side of the room, holding each other, and on the other side his family dominated the cramped space. Neither family acknowledged the other. On a dais in the centre of the room stood her intended bond mate. He wore a black gown, a darkness in contrast to her lightness. His mother helped her onto the dais opposite him. The closer she got to the man who would be her bond mate, the more her heart pounded in her chest.

He was a darkness in more than just his robe. His hair was black, cut short and tight. His features were aged but not old, as though he'd matured into a man, then the aging had just stopped. He had crinkles by his eyes from years of laughter — eyes that caught her and held her attention. Never in all of her life had she seen black eyes. They weren't scary, but watchful. He was staring at her, heating her body. Taking a breath, she stared back at him as her body awakened to the sensation of arousal. Robert Valentine might be a vampire, but her blood heated for him. She licked her lips, forcing herself to think of Katie one last time. Thoughts of her friend always stopped her thinking about anything but the protection she wanted for her.

She turned away, not liking the effect his gaze had on her body.

The priest at the head of the dais spoke. "We are here to join Sophie Ford with Robert Valentine Junior." He began to chant in a different language.

Sophie had no idea what he was saying but Robert moved closer to her. The ceremony was about to begin. She flinched when he took hold of her arms and pulled her to the centre of the circle. She couldn't help but cast one last, lingering look at the door. An escape.

But Katie appeared before her eyes, again, stilling any steps she might have made. She would never abandon her friend.

Sophie tuned in to listen.

"Who allows this union to take place?" The priest posed the question to the whole group.

"I do."

"I do."

His father and her father came forward. The priest nodded and began his chanting again.

"Is that it?" Sophie whispered. If all that needed to happen was some words, she would be able to get through this. His hands on her already offered her comfort. He hadn't grabbed her in a vicious way, but gently. So far, the vampires she'd been in the presence of had been most accommodating.

"Not yet."

Sophie turned her eyes back to the man—no, the vampire—in front of her. He closed in, trapping her against the hardness of his body.

He was so strong.

She couldn't move from the pressure of his arms.

One arm cupped her waist while the other lifted and moved her hair, exposing her neck to the crowd. Sophie stared into his eyes, mesmerised by the blackness within. She couldn't look away. She was completely in his power.

"Close your eyes," he whispered in her head.

His lips didn't move but she knew it was him talking to her. Rather than question the sanity of her situation, she did as he instructed and closed her eyes.

It seemed silly to argue with one of the most powerful vampires in the world.

Sophie could hear the chanting of the priest, the noise of the other occupants of the room, but the feeling of being close to him dominated her senses. He had no breath, no heartbeat, but she could feel him — could feel the mass of energy he produced. It was like every little warning bell inside her head going off, to caution her about what was going to happen…

Her head was tilted to the side. She swallowed down the lump of nervousness. She didn't know what to do. Her heart was pounding, the blood pumping faster through her veins.

She couldn't see, but she anticipated…

Was she nervous?

Anxious?

Excited?

Millions of tiny thoughts processed inside her mind all at the same time.

He struck.

He bit down into the side of her neck, each long tooth striking the vein. Sophie felt her blood leaving her body, leaking out. She felt him pulling hard.

She screamed. The pain was excruciating. Her life passed before her eyes — images of her life as a baby, as a toddler, as a teenager. Images of her two brothers passed. Her mother and father arguing. Christmases and summers. Her best friend, Katie. Her secret stayed buried. But Sophie had a feeling that this man — this vampire who was feeding from her — could see everything.

Her body started to go numb, the pain lessening as she lost feeling. She became light-headed and all thought left her, until she collapsed in his arms. Sophie had no strength to hold herself up. She was light and airless. Her heartbeat had slowed and she could feel her *self* beginning to leave her body. She started to spasm and knew she was close to death's door.

Suddenly—the movement jerking her body—her head was pushed into the curve of a male neck. The smell of masculine spice permeated her senses, making her mouth water. Underneath the intoxicating scent she could detect the metallic taste of blood.

She gagged, trying but failing to move. Her body wanted to live—the human instinct to survive was screaming within her. She swallowed down his blood and surrendered to the warmth, the crushing weight as he held her close.

He held her against his body, supporting her. She took what she could, feeling the power of his blood surging inside her—consuming her.

Sophie saw images of him as a boy. The whole five hundred years he had spent alive…and killing. A haze of images swam before her eyes until Sophie could take no more. She broke the contact, trying to force him away from her.

He spoke in her mind again. *Look at me.*

Sophie opened her eyes and looked at him as he took her down to the floor with him. They were both smeared with blood.

"I bind you to me, Sophie, for eternity. I am bound to protect everyone you hold dear."

Katie flashed through her mind seconds before the consuming darkness came upon her.

She passed out.

Chapter One

Three years later

"Sir? Sophie Ford is here."

Robert Valentine glanced up from his paperwork. "Well, send her in."

"Um... Sir, she's not here to see you."

Robert could feel the first stirring of his animalistic temperament.

For three years, his mate had been plaguing him.

"Who is she here to see?"

Never before had he met a woman who'd literally run out on him and not returned any of his phone calls. Who'd wanted nothing more to do with him than to ensure protection for the ones she loved.

For the first time in his existence, Robert had begun to feel jealous of humans. He had never considered himself conceited, but he knew he was a good choice for a woman. Sophie wasn't like other women. The one human female he'd been interested in and she'd all but walked out and left him stranded. Whenever he thought about her, his cock stiffened and he had to relieve himself or stay hard until her memory dissipated. Even now, hearing her name was like a direct signal to the thing in his pants.

"Well, show me her," Robert snapped, his voice harder than he had intended.

The human minion fumbled for the remote control that worked the plasma screen on the wall facing his desk. He used it to keep a vigil over everyone in the club. His minion pressed a few buttons and Sophie came onto the screen. The pen in his hand snapped from the pressure of his fist.

Sophie was in his BDSM club, dancing and humping on his dance floor in nothing more than a miniskirt and bikini top. Men crowded round her as she swayed her luscious hips. Those hips were his and his alone. He ran a hand over his face, trying to gather his thoughts, already feeling exhilaration rushing over him—a strange combination of anger and happiness.

It had been three years since he'd last seen her. The only times he'd even heard from her had been the occasional, distant phone calls she'd made. Never once had she set foot in any building he owned. Robert didn't even think she knew he owned clubs like this.

Her thoughts and feelings were pushing inside him. Having her this close was making it difficult for him to shut her out. It felt like Sophie was projecting at him, screaming for him to look up and take notice. Closing off his mind would be the only solution.

He wasn't a human adolescent male who couldn't control his urges and he wouldn't allow his mate to think he was.

She was calling for him to come and get her.

His body wanted so badly to answer that call.

"How old is she now?" he asked.

"Twenty-four, sir."

Sophie wanted his attention...and now she had it. For the last three years, he had watched and waited for her. He had known that sooner or later his blood would start to call to her. Visions of him would start to invade her every waking thought. Her dreams would be consumed by images of him. The final weakness and the test of the blood bond. Three years was a long time to wait, which proved Sophie was a strong mate. For three years, she'd rejected any chance of being with him.

Sophie had no idea of the power he held over her. The bond was only the beginning. He would own her completely when he finally took that one, precious part of her body. Her virginity was the final element of his ownership. She wouldn't be able to lie to him, then. She would be entirely at his mercy.

But Robert hated that part of the bond. The obsessive nature it created. The craziness and lust. He wanted Sophie to come to him of her own free will, not be forced by some nasty trick of nature. It wasn't right and it wasn't fair.

Still, a part of him was pleased to see her again.

"Any news from my family?" Robert got up from his chair, moving around his desk towards the door. Trying not to let his mind stray to the beautiful vision on the screen.

"Your father wants to know how it is going with Miss Ford." His minion looked down at the floor.

For three years, his father had pestered him to go and claim his mate by force. He wasn't into force and he would never take a woman in such a manner. But it would seem that his father would get what he wanted — in a manner of speaking. The mouse had finally come to him.

"Get William on the phone." Robert watched his bond mate strutting her stuff on the stage. A man held her hips in place as he thrust against her backside.

It should be his hands, should be him thrusting against her...

His brother's voice came over the speaker phone. "What's the matter, Rob?"

"Any news on Katie?" Ever since he had seen her best friend's face pass through her mind — the love and care she felt for her clear — Robert had made sure she was watched twenty-four hours a day.

Only William dared to call him Rob. He wondered if his younger brother wished for death, given the way he tried to rouse his temper. William wasn't known for keeping the peace. If anything he was usually the one to seek a fight.

Through the bond, he had no choice but to protect Katie. What his mate loved, he loved. It was plain and simple.

"Look. I have no idea why this woman is so damned special to you. Nothing. Zip. She gets up and goes to work. She's a frigging librarian, Rob. She doesn't go out during the day. She leaves in the evening, works through the night, then goes home. Her cat has more bloody fun than she does," William moaned.

"I've told you. The reason for this protection detail has something to do with Sophie's friend." Robert was sure, down to his unbeating heart, that Katie White held the answers he was seeking.

"You wouldn't think that to watch her life." William yawned. "She has to live the most boring life known to mankind."

"Keep watching her."

Robert hung up, staring at the image of his mate—willing her with all his might to spill her secrets and tell him everything he wanted to know.

Going back to his desk, he dismissed his minion and gathered up the file he'd managed to obtain on Sophie Ford. The only interesting thing about her—besides her spunk and the attitude that had been apparent at the Council three years earlier—was her bond and connection with the mysterious Katie White.

As he sat back, his mind filled with activity—a barrage of unanswered questions.

Come and get me.

Robert shot up out of his seat, looking all around himself.

I'm yours for the taking.

Rob looked at the screen. Her eyes stared right back at him. The bluest blue beckoning him to come and get her.

There was no way that she could know he could hear her thoughts.

But in truth, Robert did not care. Sophie Ford—his mate—was here, inside his club. His for the taking. And that was exactly what he was going to do.

He wasn't a fool.

He wanted his bond mate and he was going to go and take her.

Sophie could sense how close he was. Energy sizzled along her skin, making it prickle with nervous excitement. She pushed her ass along the extended shaft of the man dancing behind her, doing everything within her power to call to Robert. She didn't much care for the man she was dancing with—it wasn't his attention she was trying to get.

Her body no longer felt like her own. Most days she felt possessed, itchy and irritable in her skin. Her mind was filled with nothing but the man she was bound to. She wrapped her arms around the neck of her dance partner, her mind seemingly attuned to him—but in actual fact, her eyes sought out the vampire closing in on her. Sophie had no choices left—she needed to be able to think past this wave of lust that constantly consumed her every waking thought.

The air around her was thick and her nipples responded to the heat, budding out, pressing against her bikini bra. She had dressed to get attention and she had finally got what she wanted.

It felt like magic—her entire body was on fire. She had known at once when he entered the dance section of the club. It was like a magnetic pulse around him.

He was there on the edge of the dance floor.

Watching.

He caught her gaze and held it.

He wanted to kill the man she was dancing with. Sophie could sense his need for violence.

She didn't care. Her dance partner was a means to an end. She had wanted Robert Valentine's attention…and now she had it.

A sense of satisfaction washed over her.

She blinked and, as she opened her eyes, he was there, barely a breath away. It had been three years since the last time she'd seen him, but now he stood in front of her.

"Let her go." His gaze remained on her, but his voice held the promise of pain for her new friend.

"Buzz off, man. This girl is taken."

Sophie tensed. Of all the stupid things to say…

A second later, Robert had the butt-head pressed up against the bar, his body at a ninety-degree angle. It looked painful and Sophie winced.

"I said 'let her go,' and when I speak, you do what I say. Don't come into my club again."

Silence fell inside the club, the heavy music stopping as everyone took in the scene of vampire against human—the owner against the customer.

There were rules and this man had just broken the most important of them. Never go up against a vampire. Especially not the boss.

The man scrambled against the bar and tripped all the way to the door. Her would-be rescuer buttoned up his suit jacket, rearranged his sleeves, then looked around the room. Considering he'd just lashed out at a human in front of more than a hundred witnesses, he appeared remarkably calm and collected. Sophie couldn't help but admire him.

He gestured for the other people to continue and music filled the silence. Dancers began shaking on the dance floor and the barman continued to serve drinks, the drama of moments ago forgotten. Robert took her by the arm, forcing her along the dimly lit corridor away from people—away from witnesses. Sophie could feel the pulse in her throat.

He was angry. She could sense it.

Everyone they passed moved out of their way.

Eyes followed them. She could feel them boring into her back.

Robert Valentine dominated the entire club.

Moments later, he thrust her inside an empty room. At least, she hoped it was empty. The room was dark, with the only light coming from candles. It was small but cosy. A large bed and a cabinet filled the tiny space. The walls were painted black and the silk sheets were a deep shade of red — the colour of blood.

Swallowing past her fear, Sophie looked up at him.

His eyes were black, his body shaking with rage.

Instinctively, she took a step back.

He came forward, mirroring her every move.

"What are you doing here?" Each word was controlled as he spoke.

Sophie would have preferred the anger, the lash of his loud words. This side of him scared her more than anything had scared her in her life.

She looked away from his eyes, down at the black-carpeted floor. This entire club was so clichéd — darkness, danger and bloodshed.

This was the first time Sophie had entered his club but, now, time was of the essence. Whoever was following Katie needed to be stopped.

"I came to dance." She spoke the words to the carpet. Her heart rate increased as he trapped her against the wall. The bed was less than three feet away.

"You allowed those men to touch you." He spat the words. "Human men."

"I'm a human, Robert."

His fist connected with the wall by her head, making her jump and scream at the same time.

He wouldn't hurt her. She *knew* he wouldn't hurt her. She couldn't explain how, but it was like a natural instinct.

"You're *my* human. *Mine*." He growled the words, moments before he slammed his mouth down on hers, taking a kiss from her lips.

The move was unexpected. Sophie stood there, his lips hard against hers. His teeth had extended with his anger and they were biting into her. Yet she responded to his kiss, hands moving to hold him close to her.

She cried out as she tasted her blood on her lips, but Robert was too fast. Moments later her head was pushed to the side, exposing her neck. Sophie screamed as he bit into the delicate column of her neck. Blood rushed from her. She couldn't believe he was biting her, feeding from her. Three years, and he was taking from her without asking. She couldn't help a wave of euphoria, misplaced though it was. She knew she was supposed to be feeling angry.

He pushed his lower body against her as he drank her down. She could feel the hot press of him. Sophie suddenly felt so tired. The blood was draining from her. She couldn't move—she couldn't do anything but submit to him.

Her last thoughts were of Katie.

No matter what happened, she had to keep Katie safe.

Katie twitched the curtain.

Yep, the car was sitting in the same place as it had been an hour ago. Outside her house. The car had darkened windows. No one could look in—only the observers inside could look out. Going to work was starting to terrify her. Everywhere she looked, she was sure people were following her. The voices she heard ordering her back to her house terrified her, too.

"Come on, Sophie, pick up," Katie mumbled into her mobile phone, only for it to go to voice mail again. Groaning in frustration and temper, she placed the curtain back carefully, not wanting to alert the person in the car that she knew about them. She threw her phone onto the one remaining chair. Katie paced up and down her living room, wearing out the rug that her parents had bought years ago.

Sophie should be answering.

She picked up the phone once again and pressed the redial button, waiting for some response.

She shouldn't have allowed Sophie to go. She was on a suicide mission. Only stupid, crazy people got into bed with the vampires.

"Well, I'm the crazy one," she mumbled to herself.

Curiosity had her looking outside again. The car was still there. Swearing, Katie turned away from the window. She checked the locks on all the doors and turned the music up to full volume. Then she went in search of a map and the necklace Sophie had left when she had last stayed over.

It was dangerous and usually didn't work, but it was worth a shot. The map allowed her to see Beyer West in all its glory and the object belonging to Sophie held a connection to her. The locket she used was one she'd given her on her twelfth birthday and it was unlike Sophie to take it off…unless she didn't want to be found.

Cursing, Katie moved away from the map and held the locket. If Sophie didn't want to be found, that meant she was up to something she didn't want Katie to know about.

Indecision warred within her.

Giving up, Katie went back to the map.

She needed to find her.

Blood was being forced down her throat. Finally, the taste she had craved morning and night.

Sophie moaned in ecstasy as she took the delicious nourishment.

She opened her eyes and she began to adjust to her surroundings.

She had been with Robert in the black room with the blood-red bedding. This room was nothing like the one she remembered.

She pulled away, trying to escape. Anything that tasted this good was usually very bad for her.

"Calm down. You're in my private quarters," he soothed, moving strands of her hair away from her sweaty brow. "You need to feed."

He offered her his wrist again.

The cut dripped his tempting blood. For days she'd dreamt of being with him, and as much as she was here for Katie she was also here for herself. She'd do anything to stop the endless dreams and the sick feeling that had developed in the pit of her stomach.

Licking her lips, she gazed back at his black eyes while he offered her his wrist.

Drink or you will die.

Sophie glanced around, but the noise had come from nowhere but her head. The rolling of her stomach forced her to place a hand over her mouth.

"You have to drink, Sophie," he said.

With no other choice before her, Sophie reached out.

Keeping an eye on him, she took his wrist and began to take the sustenance she needed after so long without it.

His scent surrounded her. She could feel his blood inside her body, as hers was within him.

Sophie took as much as she could stomach, then moved away from him. After all, she was still human. Once the need had been fed, the blood tasted like blood.

But she could feel the change inside. The power and strength began to return to her. The last three years had been a struggle. With each passing month, Sophie knew she was getting weaker. Unless she ate a little food every few hours she would pass out and not remember anything of the days before. Katie had helped her to solve the mystery of her sudden tiredness. She was here not only for Katie, but for herself, too.

It would seem that part of the bond with a vampire required a constant supply of his blood. As the years went by, unless she ate constantly, her body would start to drain of energy and she would be bed-bound for weeks at a time. She didn't know why she hadn't gone to Robert—to her mate—sooner. For months she had thought something must be wrong with the blood bond. Never before had she heard of bonded couples who struggled with fatigue or illness as she did.

But other couples remained together and fed each other. The only thing missing in her case was the blood.

Robert pressed a damp cloth to her brow.

"You're ill."

Sophie couldn't argue with him and she didn't have the strength to stop him from caring about her.

Already she could feel the welcoming warmth of his blood inside her body.

"I feel better."

He nodded.

She looked at him. Really looked at him.

He wasn't handsome, but he was sexy. Confidence and power emanated from him. Just by looking at his facial features, you would know he was someone of extreme importance. He had a tan, letting her know that he wasn't restricted to the night time just because he was a vampire. His black eyes shone with knowledge. His eyes were the scariest thing about him — they followed her wherever she went. The eyes of a predator. He was strong, his body muscular. Even if he hadn't been a vampire, he would still have been a strong man. As always, though, it came down to his eyes.

No living person had black eyes.

"Why am I so weak?" she asked.

He stopped and gazed at her.

Sophie had no choice. She needed all the answers.

"You don't know?"

She shook her head. "I thought I was supposed to benefit from this bond." She sounded petulant, even to herself.

"None of your friends are dead, are they?"

"Well, no —"

"Be thankful, Sophie. Most friends take advantage of the blood bond. It seems you and Katie are very quiet."

He wrung the cloth out and wiped the blood away from her neck. Reaching up, she pressed her fingers against the bite marks.

"They are healed, but you will have the marks for some time."

Sophie nodded. There wasn't a lot she could do about it. The wounds would just have to be covered up. She might be a blood-bonded mate but she didn't have to advertise the fact.

Vampires might officially be considered citizens in this country, but there were still groups of humans trying to find new ways of killing them. Of wiping them out. People like her, who gave themselves to vampires, were considered fresh meat — the bottom of the food chain.

And though they might not like it, these groups understood the bond between vampire and human.

They knew that taking the human and torturing her would bring the vampire out into the open. They knew that by killing the blood-bonded mate they could weaken the vampire, and so those were the moments when they struck.

Vampires could survive past the severance of the blood-bond, though the human could not. But in the first moment the human was killed, the part that connected them would be torn from their bodies, shocking and weakening them. Their senses would be useless until their body had adapted.

Unluckily for her, if Robert ever died, her body would never be strong enough to survive the severing of the connection. She would die within minutes. Bloody good job it took much more to kill a powerful vampire than to kill a human.

Sophie had no plans to die in the immediate future.

"Why am I still weak after just feeding from you?" Sophie asked.

"You know about the lack of blood?" he asked.

"Kind of hard to miss that memo."

He nodded understanding.

"You will start to weaken as my blood leaves your body. It has been three years since you last fed from me and you, Sophie, need to learn to accept me again. It will take a little time before you start to feel normal." Robert wiped his hands on the towel.

"What do you mean? I thought I was strong enough with the bond and little blood." Sophie pulled herself up into a sitting position.

He sighed, shaking his head. "This is why people shouldn't get involved unless they know what they are offering."

"What? What's going on, Robert?"

"The blood bond works. You can feel me? Sense me?"

Sophie nodded.

"Well, the bond works by giving protection through the blood. Because I drank your blood, I knew who you cared for and how to protect them. By the same token, you should feel stronger and healthier and the aging process should slow down and eventually stop—but only with a constant supply of my blood."

"I don't understand. I'm getting weaker," Sophie complained.

Sophie heard him growl, then Robert looked up at her. "That is because the bond was never completed. Also, you didn't stay around long enough to take regular feedings from me."

Sophie's mind stopped working, her heart racing.

"What do you mean the bond was never completed? You drank my blood until I was almost dead. I remember. Then I drank your blood."

He pressed his finger against her lips, stopping all talk.

"That was the start of the process. To complete the blood bond, you have to give yourself to me willingly."

"But I did all that."

"No. You have to give *all* of yourself to me. There is a reason a blood bond mate has to be a virgin. I must be the first and only one."

Sophie couldn't stop her eyes from widening. "Do you mean I have… No, I mean—"

"We have to have sex. Sex, along with the blood draining, brings the connection. You will need to stay with me."

"Stay with you?" The surprises just keep on coming tonight.

"That is why you've been getting weaker. You will need my blood and I'll need yours to keep the bond strong. Always."

Sophie felther mouth open in shock.

"But, but—"

"You thought you knew all of our secrets?"

Sophie watched him get up off his seat.

"We need to have sex?"

"I gave you over three years to come to terms with this."

She shook her head. "Not sex, you didn't."

"You came to us like you knew what you were getting yourself into. I've upheld my part of the bargain and will continue to do so. However, if you don't take my blood or fulfil the blood bond, you will continue to get weaker. I don't want to upset you with all the details, but let me say it won't be pretty," Robert said, confirming the harsh reality of her situation.

Sophie ran her fingers through her hair.

"What happens if I don't agree? And don't pretty up the facts. Like you said, I came to you thinking I knew what I was getting myself into. I obviously didn't know everything, and now I'd like to know." She could feel the energy returning to her.

"These past three years, you've been getting weaker. Well, over time, you will grow weaker still. You won't be able to get out of bed in the morning. Simple tasks will become impossible. Until eventually, you'll be too weak to live. You'll go into a coma and die."

Sophie gasped. Katie couldn't have known this.

"Could I use your bathroom?" Her voice came out squeaky. She tried to control the flow of tears she felt so close to the surface. She removed the blanket, feeling the quaking in her body.

In order to survive, she would have to spend the rest of life with this vampire.

"The bathroom is through there." He pointed across to the second door.

She nodded, moving slowly away.

"There are clean bath towels."

Sophie nodded again.

She closed the door and went immediately to the shower, turning it on full blast. Next she twisted the taps on full blast in the sink. She locked the door and pulled out her mobile.

Seventeen missed calls. What could Katie want now? This whole plan was not panning out the way they'd originally planned and Sophie was starting to think it was going to backfire on them. Sophie took a deep breath to try to get her nerves under control. Katie wouldn't be able to handle hearing her one support losing it.

She pressed speed dial for Katie's number.

"Thank God. Where have you been?" Sophie could hear the fear and panic in her best friend's voice.

"I'm sorry. I've been trying to get his attention—"

"Someone is here, Sophie," Katie cut her off. "The same car is here and has been for the past week. Ever since you left."

"Oh, God." Pressing her palm to her forehead, Sophie tried to work past the fear. "Are you sure?"

"Every time I wake up the same car is there. I went to work and it was outside the library. I'm freaking out, Soph." Katie burst into tears. "Maybe you should just tell them the truth, or at least I should come in. If we cooperate, they might not kill me."

"Katie, calm down. I'll fix it." She stepped closer to the shower, hoping against hope that Robert wouldn't be able to hear her over the rushing of the water.

"We've worked too damn hard to give up now and I refuse to allow anything to happen to you. You're my best friend."

"How can you fix it? My parents told me to be careful. Never to stay in one place for too long. I should have left when I was younger. I should have sold my parents' house and just left." Katie was panicking, and when she was frightened she talked without taking a breath.

Sophie couldn't afford for her to freak out at this stage. She could hear the sound of drawers opening. Katie was packing. Sophie cursed. She didn't have time for this. Between finding out that the blood bond wasn't complete and Katie being in more danger than ever, she was close to pulling her hair out.

"Katie. Stay put. I said I'll sort it and I *mean* I'll sort it." She snapped the phone shut, not giving her friend time to argue. She prayed Katie would listen and wait it out. Sophie glanced up at her reflection in the mirror.

A pale, scared woman gazed back, confused and tired. Was his blood starting to wear thin?

The puncture wounds stood out, red and sore against the paleness of her neck. She touched them with the tip of her finger and flinched at the contact.

Katie flashed into her mind again. All this was for her.

She unbuttoned her top and took her skirt off, then jumped into the shower. She wanted to wash off the sweat and grime from the nightclub, as well as the blood and pain she had experienced with Robert.

What was the use of saving her virginity if she could save her friend instead? If she didn't give herself to Robert, she would die anyway. She should just dispense with it and think about Katie.

Her virginity should be the last of her worries, but over the years it had become the one thing she could control. No one could tell her when to relinquish it.

Though Sophie *wanted* Robert to be her first. He should be experienced enough in pleasing a woman — years as a vampire ought to have taught him something.

At least she hoped so.

Making up her mind, Sophie got out of the shower.

She would give herself to him tonight.

Chapter Two

Robert watched her go, sensing that something wasn't right. He could hear the distant sounds of her mumbling and when he searched closer with his hearing he could tell she had intentionally drowned out her voice with the noise from the shower and the water running from the tap.

Clever. So she did know some tricks of the trade.

Picking up his mobile, he dialled William for the second time that night.

"What's the update?" he asked, his gaze never leaving the bathroom door.

"Something is not right here." His brother sounded wary.

Strange, considering that only hours before he'd seemed bored with the entire process. It started to make Robert concerned.

"In what way?"

"Besides the twitching of the curtain, I've got a sense that something is about to happen."

"You had your doubts earlier this evening."

"Blame it on my bored ass. People are circling the house. Stopping and staring at her." He heard William shifting the phone from one ear to another. "She may be human, but she isn't your average human. Even if she does look like she's about to fall down dead."

"What sense do you get from the people circling?" Robert asked.

"Evil."

He tightened his grip on the mobile. If Katie was in danger, what did Sophie have to do with it? And what was she keeping from him?

"What do you think she is?"

"I don't want to talk on the phone because you know what animal hearing is like."

Robert understood immediately.

"Grab the girl and move out. This is going to get ugly." Robert was beginning to sense something and he didn't like it.

"What about you and your mate?" Robert knew what his brother was referring to. If Sophie had purposefully withheld vital pieces of information, then he would have no choice but to punish her. If he did not, then the Council would.

The thought was sobering.

He'd finally got his mate with him and he knew he could lose her again if he treated her badly. Why couldn't life as a vampire be simpler?

"I'll handle things here. You just stay safe and get the girl. Go to a safe house in the country. I don't care — just get gone." He shut his mobile and threw it onto the bed. Then he heard the shower stop. He had completed the call in the nick of time. Robert didn't want Sophie to know the danger she and her friend were in. He needed to get his anger under control. If only she'd told him the true nature of the threat the wolves posed. He couldn't alert Sophie to what he'd discovered. Through his connection with her, he already knew how close she was to Katie and telling her of the danger she was in would be a massive mistake.

He couldn't bear to think of punishing her. His gut twisted at the thought of her alone or in pain. He must—no matter what the cost—protect her at all times.

She was his blood-bonded mate. She was his reason for living and breathing...figuratively. Vampires didn't actually breathe, but with the power of the witches, years ago, they'd performed a spell to make vampires better able to appear human. So they could appear to be breathing, in the company of humans.

Robert listened as she moved around the bathroom, brushing her teeth and drying herself. If he strained his senses, he would be able to smell her natural fragrance. The innocence of her life and of her body. Sophie smelt like total heaven. He would struggle to keep his hormones in check if he didn't control himself.

He heard the door open, and there she stood. Wet and beautiful. Her blonde hair, darker now from the shower, lay down one shoulder, covering the top of her breast. Her stance was confident but her face gave away her fear.

Sophie wanted to complete the mating ceremony but she was terrified of the idea.

"Does the thought of being with the dead repulse you?" he asked. If he got her fear to the surface he would be able to control the need to go over to her, get down on his knees and beg her to keep him for all eternity.

She folded her arms over her breasts. Finally, the fire he had loved about her from the first was coming to the surface to defend her.

"You're not dead."

"Ah. To some cultures, I'm even worse than a dead person. I chose to be this way—dead but not dead. Living, but again, not living." He sat down on the edge of the bed, facing her.

"Others would argue that you have the best of both worlds," she said.

"How is that?"

"You live and you cannot die," she answered.

"I can never be in the sunlight without the aid of human blood—yours, as a matter of fact. I can be killed and I'm hunted on a daily basis by people who believe I'm the scum of the universe." He watched as she flinched. "Suddenly, my being a vampire doesn't seem so grand, does it?"

Sophie was silent but he could feel her gaze on him. He kept up the barrier, stopping himself from reading her thoughts.

"Are you evil?" she finally asked.

"No," he answered truthfully. In his mind, he wasn't evil. He was a man of honour and integrity. He didn't believe in attacking until forced to. For many centuries he hadn't killed a person by draining their blood, and he'd attacked only to protect himself or his family.

She came a little closer to the bed.

He watched and waited, not wanting to interfere, wanting to allow her to go at her own pace. If it was up to him, they'd both be naked and fucking already, but Sophie was a virgin and his mate. She deserved special attention when he finally took her for her first time.

Robert knew what she was about to do and he let her. The towel dropped. He wasn't prepared for the immediate tightening in his groin. She was spectacular. He was over five hundred years old and never before had he seen a woman quite so perfect.

She still had the rounded curve to her belly that he recalled from the ceremony. Sophie was unique in more ways than one. First, she wasn't concerned about being a size zero and she cared very deeply about the people she loved. Her stomach called to him. He could already imagine himself nibbling and biting it. Her legs were short and full, but strong. He could see the defined muscles along her thighs. Her breasts were full and pert, her nipples erect — from the cold or from her desire — red and beautiful. A flush coated her breasts, moving up to her neck. Her eyes were wide, her mouth slightly open. A tempting invitation to take, kiss and plunge inside. Her little tongue peeked out, licking lips that appeared to be getting fuller by the second.

His gaze travelled up until he met her waiting eyes.

"What do you want from me?" he asked. His voice became husky as the sight of her body had its effect on his own. His cock, which had lain dormant for three years as no woman could arouse him the way Sophie could, awoke with fresh life. He wanted to be inside his mate. The need to take her in the most primitive of ways lay beneath the surface of his skin. Vampires could react on impulse. William allowed the urge to flow over him but Robert took great pride in maintaining control. He no longer wanted to be in charge of his emotions. What would happen to him and Sophie if he allowed his natural instincts to kick in? He turned his head away so that he no longer stared into her blue eyes. Anything in the world she asked for, he'd willingly give. Cut out his own dead heart, and she could have it within seconds.

"I want the bond to be complete," she said.

It was the answer he had been expecting — she didn't know how to ask in any other way. He already knew of her innocence.

Robert took hold of her hands and pulled gently, bringing her closer to him. He could smell how turned on she was. Her light scent invaded his nostrils. The bitter taste of her fear was unwelcome, but he knew that virgins always feared their first time.

He felt her tremble but she remained before him. Her courage should be worshipped.

Robert held her hands, not moving. He looked at her, making sure she kept her eyes on him and only on him. He stroked his thumb over her hand, trying to reassure her.

Using all his willpower, he opened up the connection between them. Her eyes were the key. He forced her to watch him, to trust him. Holding her hands provided the conduit of touch and her eyes gave him the key to her mind.

He hated himself for doing this, but time was of the essence.

"What do you want from me?" Again, the picture of a smiling Katie appeared before his eyes as she spoke.

"To finish the bond." Her answer came in a dull voice. She was strong. She was fighting his hold on her. Her words seemed practiced.

No human could be this strong. He searched her mind and found the problem. He burst through the gate locking away her most hidden memories and treasures.

"What do you want from me?"

Images invaded his mind and he got his answer.

Sophie was walking in the forest with Katie.

"Andrew was so wanting to ask you out." Katie laughed as she followed Sophie.

"I didn't want to be drooled on again. I mean, the guy kisses with his mouth open." Sophie swung around the tree, laughing and happy.

"At least you get guys asking you out." Katie moved on.

Sophie stopped laughing, immediately going to comfort her friend.

"You'd get them asking you out all the time if you didn't glare and spook them out with your witchy tales. Boys are stupid, Katie. One day, someone will see how amazing you are and you'll never get rid of him even if you want to." Sophie kissed her friend on the cheek, linking her arm through Katie's as they walked.

"Knowing my luck, I'll get someone who's crazy and can't live without me," Katie played along, her voice growing dimmer.

Robert could feel how sad Sophie felt for her friend. Katie was different. Sophie knew it and so did the rest of their peers. It drove Sophie crazy. Robert sensed her anger and disappointment. If Sophie could accept Katie and her differences, why couldn't anyone else? There was a beauty to Katie and she deserved to be loved. Robert knew the bond between the two friends was like the strong bond of sisterhood.

Katie smiled, tears streaming down her face.

"You're a great friend."

"I know, Katie," Sophie teased and kissed her on the cheek again.

They held hands as they moved through the forest, their connection solid.

They walked on a little way before a snap scared them both. What happened next should have scared them even more. Katie screamed, her hands shooting out towards the sound. The tree directly in her line of sight exploded before them. As shards of broken bark scattered, Katie gasped. Standing in front of Sophie, she slammed her arms out, forcing out a protective shield that threw the shattered wood in the opposite direction.

The only sound in the forest was the erratic breathing of the two girls. Shocked, scared…amazed at what had just occurred.

Katie screamed, looking at her hands as if they had caught on fire and she didn't know how to put them out.

Sophie got up and comforted her. No fear – nothing.

"It's okay, honey, look at me." She soothed her friend, calmed her down.

Then she took charge, protecting Katie. Trying to get past the confusion. "We have to get out of here."

What the hell had just happened?

Sophie looked around one final time.

Sophie hadn't consciously registered it, but Robert saw the wolf that had stared after them. The scene changed.

"My parents are dead, Sophie, dead." Katie sounded terrified.

"I know." Sophie cuddled up next to her on the bed.

"They sent me a warning."

"What kind of warning?" Sophie stroked Katie's hair, consoling her as best she could.

"To keep my powers to myself. That they'd be coming for me."

"Who would be coming for you?"

"They didn't say! They just warned me to be careful. I'm scared, Soph."

They wrapped their arms around each other, Sophie and Katie trying to gain comfort, but both knowing that their lives had changed forever.

Robert allowed the images and the years to flicker. He realised that he'd seen Sophie at around seventeen. He searched her memories, hating himself but knowing it was what he needed to do in order to keep her safe. He'd made an oath and a blood bond to protect her and her friend. He would make certain he stuck to it.

"I can go to the Council," Sophie argued.

"Council? You mean the Vampire Council? You know what they do to people like me." Katie moved towards the window of her parents' old house.

"We don't even know what you are, Katie." Sophie moved to stand beside her friend. She placed a reassuring hand on her shoulder.

Katie shrugged her off, moving away.

Sighing, Sophie said, "Me going to the Council and requesting a blood bond –"

"Do you even know what a blood bond entails?" Katie yelled, her voice angry and scared. "You have to perform a ritual of blood swapping, Sophie! You could die! Do you even know how powerful and dangerous vampires are?"

Katie covered her eyes, trying to stem the tears.

Robert could sense, through Sophie, the burden of emotion that Katie had been under. It had been as if her powers were draining her of common sense. Consuming her until there was nothing left.

"You have to calm down."

"I am calm!" The lamp beside her exploded.

Sophie didn't move a muscle, almost as if she had been expecting it.

The years that had passed should have helped Katie to gain control of her power. Yet it seemed as if all she had done was lose more and more control over herself.

Katie fell to her knees. Her sobs filled the air, echoing off the walls. "I just want to be normal."

Sophie stood watching her.

"I'm going to the Council." Her voice allowed no room for argument.

"They'll kill me."

"Do something to lock my memories away. Create something that means my parents have to ask and I'm the payment." Sophie went over to her and, taking her elbow, she pulled her over to the sofa.

"I can't do this to you."

Sophie grasped Katie's chin. "Look at me. You're my best friend and I know you would do the same for me. Do a spell or whatever it is you do to keep my memories locked away so I can't speak them and so that my parents need this meeting – or believe they do."

"What happens if I get it wrong?"

"You won't get it wrong. Look at me, Katie…look at me. I trust you."

Robert came out of Sophie's memories with all the answers he needed. That was why Katie's face kept appearing in front of his eyes with no explanation. Katie was a full-blown witch, but with no guidance she wasn't able to understand the magic she possessed. She was out of control.

During the process he drained Sophie of all of her energy, catching her in his arms. Gently, he laid her naked on the bed. He stroked her hair away from her face.

She was in so much danger and she wouldn't even be able to comprehend what he had to do. His stomach tightened at the thought of what was to come, but first he needed to take care of business.

If only the vampire rumours about witches hadn't been spread. Rumours were the most powerful source of propaganda. Word reached out and, before anyone knew what was happening, people were believing the ghost stories. After the last witch hunt, the Vampire Council had formed and decided that, for their own protection and that of the remaining witches, it would be best to allow the world to believe vampires were behind the death of witches.

At the time, it seemed sensible to say that the vampires were taking out Earth's natural creatures, rather than to place the blame with the humans or the wolves. Witches were powerful, but vampires deadly—it would drive the few surviving witches underground, which would protect them from the real threat—the wolves. Except, like all rumours and ghost stories, it had backfired and not a single witch had been seen in centuries. They were rare and powerful beings. Katie was certainly powerful—even within Sophie's memories, Robert had been able to feel it.

He glanced down at his mate. He could feel the pull in his heart. Robert would do anything he could for this woman. He just hoped she would trust him enough to let him into her heart.

Chapter Three

Katie yelped at the sound of the door banging. The loud music did nothing to drown out the noise. It had been years since she'd last opened the door to a stranger. The knocking was hard and insistent. She hesitated at the top of the stairs. So long since she'd had any visitors. Sophie was the only person who visited her now, and she had a key.

She glanced anxiously at the clock. It was nine-thirty. Maybe if she ignored it, whoever it was would go away. She moved up another step, stopping as the knocking came again and the pounding of her heart hindered her movement. She pressed a palm against her heart, praying for the calm and peace she needed. Once the knocking stopped, her heart rate slowed and she took a couple of steps.

The knocking came again, but this time it didn't stop—it was just a constant noise. She covered her ears to try to keep out the dark. Katie was scared, and when she was scared she couldn't control her powers. She could feel the stirring of fire in the pit of her stomach. The sick, acrid taste in her mouth. Her body broke out in a sweat and she was shaking all over.

She took deep breaths with her hands covering her ears, but it was like the pounding was happening inside her head. She couldn't stop the noise. Once it had started, she must wait until it ended. Driving her crazy, constantly crazy.

"Please, stop it," she whispered.

Nothing. The pounding continued. She collapsed on the stairs, her eyes squeezed tightly shut, her hands shaking from the effort. Her head felt like it was being smashed against a brick wall.

Katie felt the burning, the fear—she wasn't in control of herself.

"Stop!" she screamed the word.

Silence landed.

"Open the door, Katie." The voice sounded from the other side of the door.

She couldn't be sure at first whether she had really heard it.

"Open the door, Katie," it came again.

"Who is it?" Her voice was hoarse from screaming.

Katie could hear movement on the other side of the door.

"Sophie Ford sent me."

Katie flew down the stairs, a smile of relief on her face. She pulled open the door…and screamed.

This was no human. He stood tall and scary on her doorstep. A sense of anger radiated off him. She went to slam the door, but he stopped her, the brute force shocking her. She tried with all her might to push the door closed, but he just opened it all the way, then calmly shut it, observing her.

"You shouldn't be able to come in here without an invitation," she accused.

"Guess what, sweet cheeks — you're not human. The rules don't apply." He shoved her out of the way, heading for the window where she'd spent the entire week twitching the curtains. "I guess that answers one question I've got. You're not normal."

"Who the hell are you?" she demanded. How dare this strange man bombard his way into her home and treat it like his own, telling her she wasn't normal?

"Stop the screeching. Yep, there they are — a full pack." He turned to glance at her. "You must be something special."

"What? N — no. You've got the wrong girl," she stuttered. "And I *am* human."

Katie was shaking inside.

"Guess again, sweet cheeks. You're not. You're not a vampire, and you're certainly not a wolf, but there is no way in hell you can be what I think you are, sweet cheeks."

"Don't call me that," she told him.

"Okay, what about doll face?"

"Be serious. Who the hell are you?"

He circled around her. "We can deal with the introductions later, darling. First, we've got to get you out of here. They're circling like a hungry pack and I've got a feeling you're on the menu. Let's get out of here in case the menu is raw, non-human female, shall we?"

Her thoughts were running in all different directions. He wasn't making an ounce of sense and she was confused.

"What?"

Then she heard the growl, moments before her front door disintegrated as a giant wolf crash-landed in her porch.

She screamed, lifting her hands to defend herself. The wolf blew up. Like all the times before, when she was afraid or angry, things went poof.

"Ah, so you can defend yourself when you're scared. Good to know," the stranger commented.

He seemed impressed.

"Incoming!" he shouted.

Another wolf came in to the house.

Before she could attempt to use her magic, he shot it.

"Silver bullets are handy, but not deadly. Has this place got a back exit?" he asked.

She nodded, leading the way. As they went she heard several more shots. Her hands were shaking so badly that when she got to the door, she couldn't turn the key. She threw her hands up and the door blew open. The first time she'd ever aimed at anything and blown up the right thing.

Her powers were so unpredictable. One of the reasons she didn't want Sophie living with her full time.

They ran out into the night. He grabbed her elbow, circling along the dirt path. She noticed that he took them along the edge, back to the front of the house. He beeped open the car she recognised as the one that had been stalking her.

She stopped.

"Get in," he ordered.

"I'm not getting into a car with you." Okay, so he'd just saved her life, but the idea was ridiculous. She would not get into a car with a vampire.

"Look, get in the car with me or go with the furry wolf. Your choice. I imagine they'll want to carry you away with their teeth, rather than in the nice little car I've got." He got into the car and waited.

She looked over at her house, seeing one of the wolves clock her. Crying in frustration, she jumped into the car with him and they roared off into the night.

She glanced behind her. The road appeared clear. Katie sank down into the seat. Strangely, she felt comfortable, the smell of leather overriding any fear she might have felt.

"Thank you."

"Don't mention it." The stranger glanced in the rear-view mirror and took a sudden right. He seemed calm and collected.

"What's your name?" she asked. A sense of safety and peace came over her.

"William Valentine."

Katie gasped.

"That's right. You and my brother's mate are in a heap of trouble. Actually, from what I've just seen, you're in a heap of shit. That is the only nice way I can say it."

Katie remained silent.

"Keeping the fact that you're a witch quiet was a really stupid idea, just so you know," he mocked her.

"I'm not a witch and, anyway, I thought witches didn't exist. All you vampires wiped them out."

They turned left this time. She grabbed onto the handle to keep herself from being flung across the car.

"Fact one—up until twenty-four hours ago, all known witches were presumed dead, their lines killed off generations ago. I guess that what with you being able to throw fire and blow things up with your bare hands, I've decided to rethink that assumption. You're the first witch I've met in a long time. Fact two—vampires never killed witches. We always worked in sync together. It was the wolves and the humans who killed off the witches." He pulled up and parked the car.

Katie paled.

"Where is the rest of your family? And don't lie — you and your friend are already in the vampire bad books." He turned to face her.

She noticed his penetrating green eyes first.

How odd. She was in danger — in running-for-her-life danger — and she was noticing how good her saviour looked. Very strange.

Considering that his whole body spoke volumes of anger and irritation, his eyes seemed friendly by contrast.

He wasn't handsome but he had a presence about him. Katie guessed that came with being over six feet tall.

"My family is dead."

"Poor you. So that explains the attempted capture tonight. They'd been checking you out. One witch is easier to capture than a whole family." He seemed to be talking to himself, so Katie stayed silent.

She didn't want any more anger aimed at her tonight.

"This is a disaster." He sighed, turning back to look out of the windscreen. He started the car back up.

"Why don't you want to kill me?"

"Like I said, you're the first witch I've seen in a long time. Our kind doesn't kill your kind."

"But the rumours and the tales —"

"All made up. Ever since vampires and witches have known of each other, we've worked together. We have a bond. We always thought it rather poetic — the undead and the magical spirit combining together." He drove slowly along a country lane.

"Where are we going?" she asked.

"To my place. It'll be safe there until I can talk to my brother," he told her.

Katie relaxed back in her seat. She'd rather be in the bad books of the Council than have to deal with a hungry pack of wolves.

"What about Sophie?"

"My brother is going to finish the bond tonight, then we'll deal with the Council."

Katie nodded, not caring whether he could see her. If the Council decided to kill her, at least Sophie would be safe through the blood bond.

She watched him manoeuvre the car down the roads and she smiled. No man had ever taken her for a drive before.

"Don't start getting moon eyes at me — I'm not my brother," he warned.

Katie chuckled. "I don't want anything from you. I was just thinking about my friend and the bond."

"I take it you're the one responsible for all that."

"No. Sophie suggested it and started to put a plan in motion. I just did what she told me. As I'm sure you know, Sophie can be very persuasive when she wants something. She likes him, you know?" Katie felt safe and happy for the first time in years. William made her feel this way. She just wanted to chat, like any girl her age.

He turned his head for a fraction of a second.

"Who?"

"Sophie. She likes your brother Robert."

He laughed. "I think he likes her, too."

They shared a smile.

Chapter Four

Sophie was dreaming. She lay beside the river, running her hand through the clear water. She could see the beautiful tropical fish and the wonders of the underwater plant life.

She wanted to stay there forever. Her mind and her body were at peace.

"You like it here."

Sophie turned to the sound of the male voice interrupting her thoughts. Robert stood there all in white, a contrast to his dark features.

She smiled, happy to see him. "It's beautiful."

He joined her, sitting behind her so that she rested between his legs. Safe and warm.

The sun shone down. This entire place seemed happy and serene.

"I could stay here forever," she sighed. She swirled the water with her hand and watched the rippling effect of her actions.

"I could stay here with you." His hand joined hers.

Together they swirled the water, creating larger ripples. His dark hand seemed huge surrounding hers, keeping her safe from the nipping of the curious fish.

A dark cloud wavered on the edge of their world.

Here she could feel his heart beat—never before had she felt so safe.

"Where is this place?" she asked. She tried to blank out the dark, looming cloud.

"I come here to think," he told her.

"We can't stay here, though." She knew where she was.

"No, this place isn't a physical world. It's where I come when I'm resting," he explained.

"In a way I'm in your dream world."

He smiled down at her. "Yes."

She looked around, taking in the truly magnificent beauty. The sunshine created a nice warmth but was not hot enough to be invasive or uncomfortable. The light breeze was refreshing and relaxing. This place was tranquil—the complete opposite of the man whose world it was.

"Will we come here again?" She hoped they would. She had no other responsibilities here—she was just Sophie Ford, and she was happy. She hadn't been happy in a long time. "What's with the black cloud?"

It seemed to be growing, getting fiercer as it approached.

"A reminder of the problems we have to face when we get back."

"Who else gets to come here?" she asked.

He smiled. "You're the first and only person allowed here."

Sophie liked that. This place was theirs and theirs alone.

The silence that descended made her tense. "I've done something bad, haven't I?" Sophie couldn't shake the sudden feeling of despair. Something had changed while she'd been here, and she didn't know what.

"Nothing we can't fix," he assured her.

The clouds rumbled.

"We have to go." Robert got up and held out his hand. She hesitated. "Trust me, Sophie. I promise I'll protect you."

Sophie nodded, placing her hand in his as he lifted her.

Sophie gasped as she was jerked out of her dream. Robert was sitting by her bedside, holding her hand. She placed a palm over her rapidly beating heart to try to steady herself.

She took her time to glance around the apartment. The problems were back, the worries, and the dull thump of a headache was starting in the back of her skull.

She groaned. "Do you have any painkillers?"

"Where does it hurt?" he asked, resting a reassuring hand on her shoulder.

She pressed her hand to her head, showing him.

"Take a drink." He presented her with his wrist, where blood gathered in a small cut above his vein.

She shook her head, the sight of the blood turning her stomach. No more blood and no more vampires—she didn't want to deal with this crap anymore.

"My blood will heal your pain, Sophie. Stop being stubborn and drink." He pressed his wrist to her mouth. Blood soaked her lips.

She could scent his blood. The first hint of metal invaded her nostrils...then it changed. It started to smell like him. Her stomach turned, not in distaste but in desire. Sophie liked the flavour of him.

She licked along the cut, drinking his blood.

The taste was pure heaven. Her hands came up to clasp his wrist to her mouth. She swallowed him down her throat, relishing the taste and feel of him inside her body.

Sophie felt the glow spread through her, the warmth causing her cheeks to flush. Blood seeped into her nipples, making them pulse, hard and erect. Between her thighs, through her slit, she felt the throb of her clit as it came alive, telling her of her desire.

The reaction of her body startled her. She thrust his hand away, covering her nakedness with the sheet, creating a little more distance from him.

"You desire me. Your body is merely responding to it." He cleaned the remainder of the blood from his wrist. The cut had already sealed itself.

She had to keep reminding herself that he was a vampire. Being around him made her forget about what he was. He acted like a human.

"That is because I was human once."

Startled, she looked at him.

She was sure she hadn't spoken aloud.

She must have. He'd never before been able to read her mind, she was sure of that. And she couldn't read his.

"I won't hurt you, Sophie."

"You're a vampire. Don't you hurt everyone?" She wanted to hurt *him*. Her emotions were all over the place. She felt betrayed, but didn't have the first clue why.

Sophie felt raw and naked. Okay, so she *was* naked, in her pathetic attempt to seduce him, but that wasn't the type of naked she was referring to.

Exposed would possibly be a better way of describing it. She scratched her head, trying to figure out what was wrong with her.

Then she was amazed to realise that the headache was gone.

She looked at him, only to see him smiling.

"I told you my blood was the best painkiller."

She smiled back. She couldn't help it. When he did smile—which wasn't often—it lit up his face. It transformed him from handsome to downright sinful. Her heart fluttered in her chest.

If he used that smile more often, she would be on her knees begging for his attention.

"Thank you," she said.

He moved up on the bed until he was directly facing her, lifting her chin with one finger. He gazed into her eyes.

"You're very welcome."

Sophie couldn't look away. The startling clearness of his eyes eased the pounding ache in her heart. The headache was gone, but her treacherous body was creating other problems, opening up and coming alive underneath his searching gaze.

It was as if her body became active when she was around him. No other man had ever created these conflicting feelings.

Sophie went from wanting to cover up and hide to wanting to drop the sheet and beg him to make love to her.

"I can smell you," he hissed.

Sophie watched as he got up from the bed and paced the room. It was a small room for such a large man to walk repeatedly in the same pattern.

There she went again, thinking of him as a man rather than a vampire.

When his words registered, Sophie couldn't stop the blush staining the tops of her breasts working its way up into her cheeks. She bowed her head, embarrassed.

She heard him curse, and moments later he was on the bed before her. Sophie watched him through lowered lashes. She could safely observe him like this.

Robert sat there and looked at her. She could feel his ardent gaze lingering on the upper swells of her breasts where they peeked from beneath the bed sheet.

Her arms began to ache. The sheet, suddenly feeling heavy, slipped from her grasp. She gazed up as she heard his growl.

The noise—primal, heat-filled—echoed around the room. The sheet had fallen away to expose her full breasts and rounded, quivering belly to his eyes.

Interested to see what he thought, she took a chance and glanced at him. His gaze was searching her body. Absorbing it. He didn't move. He just stared at her.

His pupils dilated and she watched as his eyes moved from one of her breasts to the other. They responded in kind, her nipples hardening to painful points. The knot in her stomach wound even tighter than before.

Sophie wanted...no, she *needed* him to reach across the small space separating them and touch her. She wanted to see him bend his head—without asking her permission—and suck one of her nipples into his mouth. She wanted his dark hair brushing over her naked skin. She wanted to see the darkness of his locks against her paleness.

Inside her head, she pleaded with him to take her.

Sophie closed her eyes, no longer able to look at him, hoping.

She cried out as his wet mouth sucked in her nipple. She opened her eyes. The vision before her was more beautiful and powerful than anything she could have imagined.

He circled the painful tip, flicking his tongue. She moaned as her hand moved up to grasp his soft hair.

Her legs fell wide open.

His hands went to her sides, pulling her down onto the bed until she was lying with her head resting on the pillow.

He moved over her. His erection, beneath the fabric of his trousers, thrust against her covered pelvis. She groaned as she felt how deeply he was affected by her.

His tongue went from one nipple to the other. She writhed beneath him, wanting more contact. She stirred with him, rubbing her body against his, enjoying the delightful friction they were creating between them.

Robert bit down suddenly, drawing blood from the side of her breast, and she screamed, jerking against his mouth. As his teeth pierced her flesh, she held on to his head, moving her hips faster against his shaft. She arched up into his touch, shaking her head from side to side.

Robert leant back to look at her. She saw his yearning, his struggle to remain in control. She tilted her head back and kissed him. She could taste her own blood but she didn't care—he needed her blood and she was happy to give it to him.

He returned her kiss, poking his tongue inside her mouth, and she accepted him like she wanted to accept his cock between her legs.

"Get naked, please," she begged, her fingers going to his shirt, trying to rip it off his body. His skin...she hungered to feel his skin pressed against her own.

Since their bonding three years ago, she hadn't been able to bear another man coming near her, let alone touching her intimately. The time at the bar had reflected her desperation to force Robert back into her life. Katie and she needed the protection but, more than that, she needed the vampire who'd started this hunger within her. Dancing with the man had been a means to an end. Sophie had used him.

She'd had nothing to keep her company but thoughts of him, hot flashes of fantasy that lasted only a short time, satisfying her body but never her mind.

She couldn't think of her heart. She couldn't love a vampire. She just couldn't bring herself to do it.

Robert pulled his shirt off and pressed his naked chest to hers. Their groans mingled between fervent kisses.

Although they were together, it still wasn't complete. He still had his trousers on. She wanted them off. She wanted them both naked. She moved her hands down his back, sinking her nails in as a wave of pleasure rolled through her.

Passion — blinding passion — consumed them both.

"Take these off," she asked.

Robert left her for a split second. She watched as he unbuckled his belt. There was something carnal in watching him undo his zip. Her body responded to the sound. Her pussy clenched and her clit seem to pulse as a fresh wave of desire assailed her. He wore no underwear. Her breath stopped as she got her first look at him. He was beautiful, his muscles big and bulging. He was twice the size of her, which should have terrified her, but his size made her feel safe and excited. Her gaze travelled further down. A patch of hair traced a path to his throbbing erection. She gulped. Sophie had nothing to compare it to — there had been no other men before him. But he was huge, the head of his cock flared, moisture leaking out of the tip.

She searched his eyes, trying to figure out what he was thinking.

He simply waited for her response.

Sophie didn't know what to do. On one hand, she was terrified of what she wanted—what her body craved. On the other, she was suddenly desperate to be loved, to let all her problems melt away in the arms of this man.

Her desire to feel safe and loved was stronger than her terror.

She opened her arms to receive him again.

He went back to her, pulling the cover out of his way and tossing it off the bed. She lay open to him, her arms still spread wide in invitation, ready to accept him.

He took her in his arms, moving one arm underneath her head to provide her with a cushion. It didn't matter that a cushion lay perfectly ready to rest her head. Robert wanted to be her cushion, to have her body lying on his. Sophie moved to the side so she could hug him.

He entwined their fingers as he took her lips in another kiss.

She inserted her leg between his as he held her against his body.

It might have been hours that they lay like that, kissing. Holding each other. Sophie didn't know why, but she felt like she was falling in love with him. She couldn't describe the feeling. He didn't rush to take her body—he didn't just want her virginity. Instead he touched her, learning her body and allowing her to learn his. In moments like this she could forget he was a vampire — he was just her Robert.

"You're so beautiful," he muttered against her lips.

She smiled, loving the compliment.

"Thank you." She didn't know what else to say.

He kissed her again to soothe her. He curved his hand over her stomach. He touched her everywhere.

"You're so small."

"Only because you're so big."

She trailed kisses along his neck.

He moaned.

The ringing of the telephone pulled them both back to reality. For that period of time it had been like they'd forgotten about the outside world.

"I have to answer that." He kissed her one last time, then moved over to the phone.

Sophie retrieved the covers and pulled them over her body, suddenly feeling a chill in the air.

This was bad news — she could sense it.

Robert cursed when he saw William's name flash up on the screen of his mobile phone.

"What?" he growled. William had interrupted his time with Sophie.

"What? Don't take that tone with me, oh big, powerful brother. You haven't got the first clue about the problems I've had tonight and I'm not fucking happy." William stopped and Robert heard his brother swallowed a drink. He guessed it would be the strongest whisky he owned.

"What's the problem?"

"Problem? Which problem would that be? The one where your mate is in the shit with the Council for keeping secrets, or the problem of where she's been hiding a first-generation witch?" William stopped, allowing his revelation to sink in.

Robert tensed. "How is this possible?"

"Katie, the little friend. It would seem Sophie has been hiding one of the most powerful witches left in the world."

"Where is she?"

"Passed out on my sofa. The magic she's used tonight has drained her. She's untrained and has been left in the world un-nurtured. She has no control over what she does."

"What have you seen?" Robert turned his back on Sophie. She had sat up and was trying to listen to the call.

This was the reality. The place where they'd been moments before was a dream.

"Well, this brings us to another problem." Robert heard William pour himself another drink. "The wolves know of her existence and they attacked tonight. Her powers are strong. She blew up a wolf."

Robert swore. She was powerful and uncontrolled, which could only mean she was unstable. The Council would have to choose between having her locked away or killed. An unstable witch was the worst thing in the world.

They were up shit creek all right.

"She wants to see Sophie," William said.

"You know I can't allow that."

"We can't kill her, Robert." There was something in William's tone.

"Why?"

"She's the answer to finally ridding the world of the wolves."

Robert doubted that was all that was on his brother's mind, but he let it slide for the time being. They had more important things to deal with.

"Do you think the Council knows this?" Robert glanced over his shoulder to see Sophie tense and waiting.

"Yes. I got a call asking about the rumour of a witch. I told them you'd bring them up to speed." William took another long drink.

"I've got to take this call. Stay here," Robert ordered Sophie. He left when she gave a slight nod of the head.

He moved to his study, shutting the door before he sat down at his desk.

"You know, after what you've just told me, that they'll kill Katie and punish Sophie." He could speak bluntly now. He was out of earshot.

"Yes. You also know there is a way around that," William pointed out.

"That can't guarantee—"

"Look, we both know that the Council will not take extreme action if you and Sophie are fully bonded. You want her, otherwise, you wouldn't have agreed to this. Katie is the first witch we've seen in generations—"

"But her magic is unpredictable," Robert interrupted.

"She was alone in the world when her powers came to fruition. With training and guidance, she could be helped," William reasoned.

"You would have to agree to be with her, William. To have that link to a witch. Not only would you be opening yourself up to another witch, but you would be bonded to her for life. It would be the only way the Council would accept it. Fully bonded mates, where you took sole responsibility for her. Could you cope with such a connection after Emma?"

At the other end of the phone, Robert heard the shattering of glass. William had smashed the bottle.

"Emma has nothing to do with this. I'll do it, but don't be thinking that I want anything more from Katie than her help in fighting this war."

Robert said nothing, but he knew William and the demons he'd been fighting for far too long.

"Get your witch up to speed. I'll sort this out. You know they'll be punished, I can't stop that," Robert reminded him. His power against the Council was limited.

"But you can stop them being killed."

"Take care, brother."

"Happy mating."

The call ended. Robert threw his phone against the wall, the small device smashing under the force of his anger.

Chapter Five

An empty warehouse, somewhere in Beyer West

"She got away, sir." The soldier bowed, going onto his knees, asking for
forgiveness.

James, the leader and the greatest power among their pack, let out a ferocious growl and lashed out, and the soldier before him was no more. James was brutal—the pieces of the soldier lay spread around them on the ground as if he'd never been alive.

"I wanted that witch. What part of that statement did you mongrels not understand?" His voice carried along the ranks of his army, an army of both men and women, pure-bred wolves and mongrels—mongrels had originally been humans, who had been made into wolves by a ferocious bite from a pure-bred wolf—strong and weak. The thing with mongrels was, they were stronger than humans but weaker than any pure immortal.

One of them dared to raise a hand. James moved, his speed and presence obviously scaring the young man who would dare to interrupt while he was speaking.

"What could you possibly have to say to me right this second? You failed me. You failed me and you failed in your mission."

A whimper escaped the young man.

"There was someone else there, my leader."

James turned to the female guard who had spoken.

He walked over to her and shot out his hand to squeeze her neck. What he had learnt early on was to show these bastards that he didn't accept weakness. They did as they were told or would forever suffer the consequences.

She didn't flinch; her gaze never wavered. She stared at him with respect. He liked that—he deserved respect.

"What did you say to me?"

His anger was in control…barely.

"A vampire was there, sir." She spat the word 'vampire'.

He released her and glanced around the room. "Did anyone manage to see who this *vampire* was?"

The room was silent for a moment.

"It was a Valentine, sir."

He growled at the room. 'Valentine' was a disgusting word among his kind.

"Which one?" There were four Valentine brothers.

"William, sir."

They knew all the family—they had detailed files on every member.

"How did they know about the witch?"

"We don't know, sir."

James sneered at them. "Don't any of you read the reports? Three years ago, a Miss Sophie Ford was offered up to the Valentines by her parents as payment for protection." He circled the group, reciting his information. "Up until that time, the Fords had been a prosperous and established family. Overnight, their millions just went. It was completely unexplained. The humans believed it was down to bad business decisions and gambling, but the head of the Ford family has never gambled in his life. Magic provided this cover." Mumbles erupted among the group.

"What do you mean?" one of the soldiers called out.

"What I mean is that Katie, the witch you failed to obtain for me, cast a spell that rid the Ford family of all of their money. Overnight, it was like a global recession but for just one family—everything gone. Only, if you look at all the correct figures, it shouldn't have been possible. I don't know why the witch did it, but I'm betting it had something to do with the protection provided by the Valentine blood bond that just so happens to be with her best friend."

James had spent years trying to understand what had suddenly gone wrong. The Fords were a human family, but a powerful one. One he could have used if it hadn't been for the fucking Valentines and the bastard interfering witch.

"Your key to understanding why William Valentine was anywhere near the witch—besides his personal history—is that Sophie Ford is the bond mate of Robert Valentine. Sophie was the payment to provide protection for the witch. Now that witch is in the company of vampires. Find her and kill her or get her to me."

He left the warehouse, his guards following close behind. His plans wouldn't work without the witch. All of the wolves would answer to him if they didn't capture her soon. The Valentines were always ruining his plans. He couldn't wait to see every last one of them fucking dead. Turning behind him, he glanced at the array of soldiers about to move out.

"Oh, and if any of you get the chance…kill one of the Valentines."

Chapter Six

Sophie heard a crash seconds before Robert reappeared in the doorway.

She could tell by his expression that he was angry. She swallowed past the lump of fear building up in her throat.

"What's the matter?" she croaked.

He glared at her. "Do you have any idea of the problems you and your little friend have caused?"

He began his endless pacing again.

Sophie tensed. She didn't know what to do in these situations. The only thing she'd been thinking about was protecting Katie. Katie—she still had to keep her safe and so her lie would continue.

"I don't know what you mean," she said, before she could stop herself.

He charged over, terrifying her. She flinched away from him but he caught her.

"Don't lie to me."

He lifted her off the bed, making her face him so he wouldn't be towering over her.

"Why didn't you come to me? I could have prevented all of this. Protected you. That was my job."

She shook her head.

"Katie is a first-generation witch and you've been hiding her from me."

Sophie paled, unsure what to do or say.

"She was attacked tonight. William—my brother— saved her. She blew up a wolf, Sophie—a wolf. You came to the Council for protection. I saw your memories. I understand why you did it. I understand that you wanted to protect your friend. What I don't understand is why you'd keep from me the reason she *needed* protection. Why didn't you tell me she was a witch?"

Sophie was shaking as each revelation came to light.

"Is Katie okay?" she asked.

"Katie is fine…for now."

"I didn't know she was a witch. We knew she was different, but not that she was a witch. We wondered, but…witches don't exist," Sophie tried to explain.

Robert cursed. They'd been terrified young women, unsure what was happening, searching for some protection.

"I'll have to take you before the Council—"

Sophie was shaking her head. "They'll kill her."

"There is a way." That got her attention. "You'll both be punished, but I can stop them from killing either of you."

"I'm listening."

"We complete the bond. Once the bond is finished, you will be my mate and by the laws set out I will have to follow through in protecting you and Katie."

"We complete the bond… That means we have sex."

"We connect with each other and share blood." Robert tucked a strand of hair behind her ear. "This is the only way — trust me."

Sophie nodded. "When should we finalise the ritual... I mean, bond?"

"Tonight."

* * * *

Katie woke up crying, her hands shooting out to ward off her fear. The coffee table blew up. She screamed at the noise, startled. Next to go was a sofa. That was why, in her small house, she only had minimal furniture.

"Hey, hey. That stuff is vintage." William trapped her hands together with his.

She screamed again. She didn't know where she was and she was panicking.

The clock exploded.

"Shit."

William kissed her. So unprepared was she for the kiss that Katie melted beneath the onslaught. His lips, firm to the touch, brushed over hers. Katie didn't know if her lips were soft, but she welcomed the gentle press of his.

This was her first kiss. She didn't know whether she liked it. She hadn't been prepared for it and by the time she was ready to deal with it he had moved away. Katie wanted to reach out and ask him to kiss her once more. She wanted to know whether she liked kissing or if she wanted to be kissed. But William Valentine was not a man you begged attention from, even if she did like the way he spoke and looked.

"The best way to deal with a witch is to confuse her with kisses." The vampire in front of her gave her a cheeky smile.

Ashamed of her reaction, she lashed out at him, but he caught her fists in his hands. She would love to see how he reacted to being blown up instead.

"Be careful. I bite as well," he warned, flashing his fangs.

Katie wasn't repulsed by the pointed teeth — if anything she was intrigued by them. Was it because she was a witch, and in a way understood his differences? She didn't care.

Katie flung herself away from him.

"You disgusting monster."

"Uncontrollable witch," he retorted.

Katie couldn't help it. She lashed out again, but he was too fast and too strong. He dodged her hits, then grabbed her flailing fists, stopping her attack altogether. A battle of wills. Katie had never fought anyone who was as strong as she was. In truth, the only thing she'd managed to destroy in her whole life was the odd clock and vintage sofa.

"You're a fiery one, all right."

Fuming at her inability to hurt him, she pulled away and stormed into his kitchen. The only way she could think of to dispel the growing tensions was to walk away.

"Oh, no you don't." He stopped her as she reached for his coffee pot.

"What have I done now?"

"Besides turn my life upside down? Until you gain some modicum of control over your hands, stay away from the coffee pot." He pushed her out of the way and proceeded to make up a pot of coffee. In no time at all, the rich aroma filled the house, calming her nerves.

Katie sat down at the table and watched him moving around his kitchen. He filled two mugs with coffee.

"Cream and sugar?" he asked.

She nodded. He handed her a steaming cup. It was too hot to drink so she balanced it between her numb fingers.

"I thought vampires only drank blood," she said, to fill the silence.

"I thought humans were nice—I've since learnt differently." He appeared to have a witty retort for everything. He didn't seem bothered by the heat, and drank some of the steaming brew immediately.

"Sorry. I was just making conversation." She looked down into her coffee.

She heard him sigh. "Drinking blood keeps us strong, but we don't need it every day. Depends on how strong the person we feed from is, the connection to that person. It's very long-winded and I don't feel like talking about it." He took a sip of his coffee.

"Am I human?" she enquired.

He remained silent until she looked up.

"Well, am I?" she asked again.

"It's not a simple yes or no answer," he finally said.

Katie frowned. "How can it not be a simple answer?"

"Witches, like vampires and werewolves, existed even before humans. Witchcraft is different from coven to person to family. Magic isn't straightforward. I'm a vampire, which is pretty simple—I kill things. Witches love being complex. In fact, I don't think I've ever met a witch who wasn't a pain in the ass."

Katie took a sip of coffee, trying to absorb what he'd just said, ignoring his insults.

"I still don't know what you mean."

"Okay. If you have a witch who is a direct descendent of…say, the devil himself, you'd naturally expect that witch to be evil. But the thing with witchcraft is that, no matter what, there needs to be a balance of power. Like vampires. We're the undead—we are neither dead nor living, so we have a natural balance. Werewolves are neither a wolf nor a human, and that balance limits their power. Witchcraft is tricky, because the balance depends on the individual."

He gave her time for all the information to sink in.

"So a witch has to be equally good and bad?"

"Yes. The magic needs a balance to sustain itself. With that balance, witches can survive an eternity in which they never age or weaken."

"What happens to a witch who isn't balanced?"

"The power consumes them until there is nothing left of the person. In other words, they burn themselves out. It's like one minute they're there and the next they're a dead shell. But again it is always different. Some take a while to burn out." He stopped, turning away.

"What happens to cause imbalance?" she asked.

"We've been in a long-running battle with the wolves. They are destroying the balance by breeding humans—better known as mongrels—into the clan."

"Humans that have been turned into werewolves?"

"Yes. Natural-born werewolves were like that from birth. Consider it an extra piece of genetic code."

Katie watched him refill her cup. "The wolves are disrupting the balance."

"Yes, and so the battle between the kinds commenced. Wolves have been wiping out witches and vampires for centuries. The furry little bastards have remained in hiding for a while. We knew they were in Beyer West, but unfortunately we've not been able to find them. The fact that wolves can adapt to live among humans has made it easier for them to hunt witches."

"That's why the vampires and the witches work together?"

"Yes. May I say, you're an excellent student?"

Katie beamed a smile.

"Witches have died in this fight. When they take on a pack, they use a massive amount of magic. They live on the balance of natural forces but in battle they pick up reserves of magic—both good and evil. It's too much to balance. The body simply can't cope. The witch might kill her opponents...but then she dies." He choked out the last bit.

Katie watched as he reached into one of his cupboards for the brandy bottle, opened it and took a huge gulp. She winced, knowing what the powerful liquor could do. Many months ago she'd tried the same medicine, only to be left with a bad head, upset stomach and a bitter taste in her mouth.

"What about me?"

"What did your parents tell you?" he asked, still with his back to her.

"I kept my magic from them. It wasn't until they died that they told me it wasn't safe. I haven't been able to control it and it just gets worse."

William nodded. "I take it they visited you in a dream because, you know, dead people walking around is going to get a lot of attention."

"It was left in a note. A note and a film. They'd taped themselves. Bizarre, really, I know. What's going to happen to me?" She knew that it was going to be something bad. The news that vampires didn't hunt witches to kill them had been a relief, but it didn't change the deceit Sophie and she had perpetrated. Katie had been right, she should have just answered to the Council, then she wouldn't have to be worried about Sophie.

He turned to her then. "Do you want to live?"

What a strange question. She nodded. "Of course I do."

He took the cup from her hands, helped her from her seat. He moved the hair away from her neck. Every touch made her gasp. Her nipples budded and goose bumps erupted on her flesh. "Do you trust me?"

She shook her head.

"Good!"

He bit down into her delicate, exposed throat. Katie screamed, fighting to get away from him. William was feeding from her. She could feel the blood leaving her body. The strike from his teeth sunk into her neck. The points dug all the way into her collarbone. He would break her in two.

"Let go, please," she begged, the pain unbearable. The sounds in the kitchen were of his sucking and her whimpers.

He was taking too much.

It hurt.

Little dots were playing in her vision. She was struggling to stay awake. Her body tensed.

The pulling on her blood became too painful.

Fading…fading…fading.

Chapter Seven

Robert looked at the clock. William should be doing his bit to keep Katie safe. Now it was his turn. He drank down his shot of vodka. It would stem the fiery attraction coursing through his veins.

Robert was amazed by her bravery. He admired her. She'd had to deal with so much, terrified, scared and alone, with no one to run to for comfort, or to ask what she should do. And now he was going to complete the final part of the blood bond.

He needed to remember that Sophie was a virgin, and that in order for this to work she had to accept him into her mind *and* her body.

He glanced at the clock again. No matter how many times he stared at it, it wouldn't change what he had to do. It would be easier if he could be angry.

But two women hadn't understood the consequences of being afraid. All they had done was try to keep themselves safe.

It wasn't a coincidence that tonight had been the night the wolves had planned their attack. They still had time to change Katie to their side.

Innocence was so over-rated. If Katie had gone out and slept around, it would have just been a direct hit tonight. A quick, clean kill. But because her precious virginity remained intact, they still had a chance to manipulate her. To turn her into a mongrel-witch. No matter how much he dwelt on it, it wouldn't change the fact that Katie was innocent and at risk. He couldn't help her now.

But he could save Sophie—he just prayed he could protect her against the wrath of the Council as well. Sophie was his one and only priority. He would have to trust in William. He gulped down some of his aged brandy and turned to the door.

He entered the bedroom to see she was already in bed. She lay facing the window. The full moon shone down, highlighting her perfect face.

"You know, I've spent years thinking about this moment. Wondering if I would do it with my husband or with a friend or someone I loved." As she spoke, her gaze never left the beauty of the full moon.

"I'm sorry." He didn't know what else to say.

She rolled over to look at him.

"I'm pleased my first time is with you. I know we don't know a lot about each other and I've caused you many problems but...well, I'm happy it's with you." Sophie got up out of the bed and moved towards him.

She took his hands, bringing them up to her lips, and kissed them.

"You're my husband. Since we bonded, I've felt a part of you. For the past three years. After tonight, I don't want to be parted from you again." She kissed the inside of his wrist. "I know I've done wrong, but I did it thinking only of doing the right thing. I can't be sorry, because I wouldn't be here otherwise." She laid his palm against her breast.

He cupped her breasts, feeling the hard nipples pressing against his skin, her pale mounds filling his hands.

With one hand still pressed to her breast, he used the other to take her chin. "Your words mean a great deal to me, Sophie Ford, and there is nowhere else I'd rather be." He leant down and kissed her on the lips.

She responded to him, curving her hands around his neck. The kiss was hot, appealing to both senses, touch and taste. Sophie squirmed to get closer. To feel the contact of skin to skin. His palm never left her breast. He stroked the turgid nipple with his thumb, causing her to cry out. She opened her mouth on a scream and he plundered it, taking full advantage of her vulnerable lips. He filled her with his tongue, tasting her, exploring her.

He fisted his hand in her hair, holding her to him. Her nipples pulsed for more attention. She moaned, lifting her leg up over his hip, trying to get more intimate contact. The warm glow of lust consumed them both. They were drugged. They fed from each other's kisses. Sophie couldn't get enough of him.

He walked them backwards until they fell onto the bed.

She giggled as he landed on top of her, knocking the wind from her.

"You're heavy."

He laughed, piercing her heart with his sinful smile. She gasped as lightning shot straight through to her clit. She was doomed if that was her reaction to just his smile. There was no way Sophie would survive the main event.

He came off her, but pulled her up so that she was resting against the pillows again. He laid a kiss on her lips, then went down to her jaw and over her collarbone, making her gasp at the violent sensations running through her. She didn't know whether to pull away or beg him for more. Her body was filled with an urgency to feel this man's body between her thighs.

She opened her legs willingly, silently begging him to move between them and assuage this terrible ache, to sate them both.

Sophie was beginning to understand why people became addicted to sex.

His lips left a trail of fiery ecstasy in their wake. Her body was alive and screaming for attention. His lips were at her breasts.

"Give them to me."

She looked at him, dazed and confused.

What does he mean?

"Offer me a breast," he told her. It was strange, as though he was reading her mind.

Taking one of her mounds in her palm, she offered him a bite. She tensed, scared, but she wanted to feel him biting into her, feeding on her blood.

He teased her nipple, playing with her body.

She watched as he attended to her, his tongue flicking out. Her breasts looked wet and swollen in the moonlight.

"Bite me," she begged him.

He bit down into her nipple and she watched him swallow. The pain was light, its sting delightful. Her nipples were so sensitive, taking a pulsing message down to her clit. She could feel the gathering orgasm she'd experienced many times before — but only at her own hand.

She wanted to feel his hand between her legs. To know what it was like to have a male finger teasing her aching clit.

She took his hand and guided it to where she'd been thinking about having it seconds earlier, to where she craved his touch, pressing one of his fingers against her swollen clit. Sophie moaned and prayed he would give her more.

The merest contact had her almost dizzy with longing. She pushed her hand on top of his and she could already feel how wet she was for him. She should probably be embarrassed, but being embarrassed would take too much energy. Her energy was reserved for him.

"What do you want from me?" he asked her.

She looked up as his mouth left her breast, the cool air sending shivers down her spine.

"I want you to make love to me. To show me what it's like to be a proper woman. Your woman," she spoke the truth.

He stared at her for some time before she felt his finger move between her legs. She took her hand from over his, knowing he wouldn't do anything to harm her.

Sophie opened her legs wider so he could have complete access to her body. Her eyes closed of their own accord as she allowed her heart, mind, body and soul to be taken over by rapturous bliss.

Robert watched her give herself over to him. She looked so stunning that she took his breath away. Or rather, she would have taken his breath away if he could breathe. Her bud, peeking out from its hood, was swollen and begging for attention.

The smallest touch had her arching up to meet him, a cry escaping from her lips. He smiled. He loved the feeling of being able to take her past the point of no return. Robert didn't just want to do that with his fingers. He wanted to take the time to explore and taste her.

He moved down the bed, his gaze directly on her mound. The hairs were light blonde, giving a clear view as if she was shaved. Already her lips were filled with blood and opened wide. He could see her cum glistening all over, lubricating her—preparing her body to receive his. Her clit caught his eye, swollen, engorged and pulsing. He pressed his tongue against it, licking her. She smelt and tasted delicious.

He licked her up, her essence addictive. He'd been so long without a woman—over three years, to be exact. After the bonding ceremony, the thought of touching another woman had repulsed him. The connection between Sophie and him had been strong from the beginning. No matter what he was doing, he had always been able to sense her.

"Hold on to the frame," he told her. He'd seen her clenching her fists and, if his assessment was right, as well as never having had a man between her thighs with his cock, a man's tongue was new to her as well. This would drive her to the pinnacle in a matter of moments.

He wanted to spend as much time as he could arousing her, so that when he took her virginity the pain would be slight.

Robert spread her lips open with his thumbs. He tongued her clit, sliding up and down her slit. He licked her clean, then teased her clit again, creating more of her cream. He could see the hold she had on the bed. Her head was flung backwards, her groin moving in time with the rhythm of his tongue. He smiled as she squirmed and growled in frustration when he stopped her building towards the desired peak.

As she felt the rising climax within her, her stomach sucked in and he could see the orgasm gathering — then he pulled away, exploring the rest of her pussy. There was more to a woman than breasts and a clit. He teased the fine hairs surrounding her pussy. A little closer and he would feel the wetness of her slit, not from his licking but from her own cream. Her arousal intensifying with each caress. She appeared to be sensitive — everywhere he touched elicited a response from her.

He smiled when she moaned once again, her body and her thrusts becoming more frenzied as he refused her more of what she wanted.

His cock was tight and begging for him to plunge inside her body, but he wanted this to last. A woman's first time should always be memorable as the beautiful force it was.

"Please," she gasped when she couldn't take any more. "Please, let me come."

Her body was on fire and he would need to put the flames out soon — otherwise he would spoil the moment.

He flicked his tongue over her clit, teasing and tormenting, keeping his attention on her.

As she climaxed, he felt the response of her body, sensed the rush of endorphins pulsing through her blood. He heard it, too, as she screamed her completion into the room.

Her body jerked against the continuing onslaught of his tongue. He saw and tasted the cream leaking from her body.

Robert had the male satisfaction of knowing he'd been the first to bring her to orgasm with the use of his tongue.

Soon she was moaning for him to stop, but he refused. She had wanted orgasm and he would give it to her—multiple orgasms.

Before long, her body hurtled into another orgasm, leaving her faint and sated. Only when Robert was satisfied that she would be able to take him inside her body without pain did he move up the bed.

She opened her eyes. "Thank you."

"You're welcome, my mate." He slid along her body. Taking his cock in his hand, he pressed it against her entrance.

"This may sting a little, but I want you to look at me and never let go," he told her.

She circled her arms around his neck, connecting them further with her touch.

He guided himself into her slick entrance. He didn't look away. When his cock was in far enough that he didn't have to hold on, he moved his hand out of the way, placing it near her head.

"I'm sorry," was all he said before he jerked his hips, embedding his shaft right to the hilt inside her pussy.

Sophie screamed but she held on to him and didn't look away from his eyes. He saw the pain she felt and he felt it too, in his heart and soul. He hated causing her pain and it almost undid him. But he couldn't stop. If he didn't complete inside her body and feed from her, they would be able to take her away from him forever, and that would be more unbearable than the few seconds of pain she was going through. At least he tried to tell himself that.

"Are you all right?" he croaked.

She nodded, the action jerky but reassuring.

He moved, pulling himself all the way out, slowly allowing her to become accustomed to his strength and size. He wasn't small and she was.

"Tell me if it hurts."

She nodded, not able to find the words, he assumed.

He thrust back inside her. Her eyes widened.

He stopped abruptly.

"Have I hurt you?" Robert panicked. He needed to complete the ritual but he wouldn't be able to if she was in pain. As much as the pain of losing her would hurt him, in this moment, with her pain clear on her face, he couldn't be responsible for bringing her more. He was torn between doing the right thing and risking his very life source.

She shook her head but no words came out. Robert refused to move. He needed to make sure she was all right.

"I feel so full," she said.

He chuckled, resting his forehead against hers.

"It feels wonderful," she gasped as the jerks of his laughter sent shock waves through her pussy.

"It can feel better."

They were his final words before he took her on a journey of sexual pleasure. He pulled out of her body before plunging back inside her, going further and deeper with every stroke. He lifted her left leg over his hip, angling her pelvis so that he could go further inside her. Sophie cried out. Robert made sure to hold her on the edge between unbearable pleasure and pain. He knew he was large, thick and deeply seated inside her. Robert had spent so much time thinking about how it would feel to be inside her cunt. So many restless nights of fucking his own hand when all he wanted to do was be with this woman. The woman who would be his for the rest of his life. Her pussy contracted around him and he forced himself to hold back, to give her more time before he plunged into her wet heat.

Robert swivelled his hips, the movement nudging her clit, making her jerk in his hold.

He took her lips in a searing kiss. She scoured his back with her nails. His thrusts increased in speed. He could feel the heat building between them. He wanted to bring her to orgasm at least once with his cock embedded inside her. He wanted to feel each pulse and quiver. He wanted to know the heights of pleasure he could bring her to.

"It's too much," she panted. Breaking away from his lips, she tried to push him off her as the pleasure became too intense.

"Let it come," he urged.

He smiled as she began to push up, meeting him thrust for thrust. Her skin glowed and her cream dripped around his cock, letting him know the rapture she was feeling. Sophie was so close to the edge of release, he knew how to bring her to the final earth-shattering climax. He would never have Sophie question his skills in the bedroom department if he could help it.

As he felt her pussy flutter around his thick shaft, he spoke the binding words. "I, Robert Valentine, take Sophie Ford as my bond mate for all eternity, and will let nothing part us. By blood, by love and by all things pure, I cement her to me for life." He bit into her neck, sealing the bond with her blood.

Bright light shone around them as the blood bond was accepted and cemented by the natural forces of the earth. Sophie Ford was his and Robert Valentine was hers.

They were catapulted into a world of love and pleasure, the driving force their need for one another. Robert felt her pulse around him mere seconds before his seed erupted inside her body, burning a pathway into her heart and soul.

Her body would recognise none but his. Her blood would feed and nurture him.

Their minds connected, their souls mingled and their bodies collapsed, sated.

Sophie could feel everything. His breathing against her neck and how much her body had pleased him. She sensed him in the deepest part of her mind.

"I love you," whispered across her temple.

One of the first times she'd heard his voice had been on the ceremonial dais but the voice had been faint. She jerked as she recognised his voice, but again he hadn't spoken out loud. Only now his voice was clearer and she couldn't question what she'd heard.

She looked across to see him watching her with his black eyes.

"How?"

He stroked her face, her cheek. She could see from his expression how much he cared for her.

"You were always supposed to be mine."

Her heart jolted inside her rib cage. She stopped his hand on her face.

"What?" she asked again. Her mind was a whirl of activity.

"The force of nature has deemed you suitable to be my life's mate. The connection is there because of how well we fit together. You may not know or believe it yet, but you love me, too."

She started to protest but he paused her with a finger to her lips.

"Your mind may not accept it but your heart has awoken for me as have your body and soul. You can feel it and soon you'll accept it."

Hours later Sophie lay awake, thinking of his words. They didn't terrify her. They soothed her. For the first time in her life, she had a protector to love and care for her. She glanced over at her sleeping vampire. He looked so calm and serene, but her body awoke at the thought of feeling him inside her again. He was becoming a drug for her aching body.

Did she love this man — this vampire?

She didn't know. He intrigued her and throughout the past three years, when she hadn't been petrified for herself and for Katie, her thoughts had always gone to him. She moved the hair off his face, enjoying the softness on her fingers. She couldn't believe she was now a woman. This man had turned her from a girl into his woman.

This vampire.

Her vampire.

She smiled as he mumbled in his sleep.

"You're going to be the death of me, Sophie." He moved closer, for her to touch him.

She laughed. "It's a good job you're a vampire and will come back to me."

She giggled as he rolled over in the bed and within seconds had her trapped underneath him.

"Wow, look at how powerful and wonderful you are," she teased, surrendering to him.

She offered her lips for a kiss. He took what she gave, taking her lips for more. She moaned as she tasted him. All her senses were heightened. His smell. His flavour. Her body was alive.

"How can you taste so good?" she said when he broke the kiss.

"Do I taste better than chocolate?" he asked.

She smiled as he landed kisses on all her sensitive areas.

"Much better than chocolate," she admitted.

She let out a gasp when he stroked a sensitive spot on her neck with his lips. She arched, exposing her throat to more of his passionate kisses.

"What about ice-cream?" he teased, leaving her neck to travel to her swollen breasts.

She nodded, unable to form words. She watched his dark head as he took a beaded nipple into his mouth, nipping her slightly. Her breasts were so sensitive, a wave of bliss set off contractions inside her pussy, making her want more.

"Answer me." She felt one of his fingers thrust inside her wet channel as his teeth did wicked things to her breasts.

"Yes," she managed, her hands going instinctively for the headboard, her eyes closing of their own accord.

"What's your favourite colour?" he asked.

She shook her head, trying to think past the dizzying heights of arousal.

"Why?"

"What better chance to get to know you than in bed?"

She chuckled. "Red. My favourite colour is red."

She opened her eyes, looking down at him.

"Yours?"

"Green."

"I only eat green sweets," she admitted.

He laughed at her confession.

"Why?"

"I figure they're healthier, since vegetables are green."

Robert laughed.

How bizarre—they were getting to know each other while on the verge of making love.

"I eat any type of sweet," he answered.

"I bet."

"I can't help it. I have a sweet tooth." He removed his finger from her dripping channel and brought it to his lips, tasting her.

Sophie flushed at the suggestive act.

"How do I taste?" she couldn't help but ask.

"Sweet."

She smiled.

"I'm going to make love to you," he informed her.

Sophie lay still and surrendered to his masterful skill.

He took her on a rollercoaster ride that seemed to have no beginning and no end. Nothing mattered—not Katie, not the Council, not even the fact he was a vampire. Sophie was content to be in his arms.

Once he had brought her to the peak of ecstasy, balancing her on the edge until he guided her over into her climax, he followed soon afterwards.

She lay spent, her mind starting to accept that she just might be falling in love with her mate.

Chapter Eight

William watched as Katie woke up, her cheeks regaining their colour. His blood mixed with hers would give her some control over her powers and would give them some leverage with the Council. He hated those fucking uptight bastards. They didn't know what it meant to experience loss. His father could talk the talk but as far as he was concerned he'd never had to deal with the shit.

William spent as much time as possible trying to stay away from the fight and the political crap the Council were spilling, but no matter what he tried to do he always got sucked back in.

He glanced down at his wrist watch. Time was ticking and Robert should be at the Council meeting by now. Part of him wanted to say stuff it. Take the witch and make a run for it. Katie was too valuable and precious to give her up to the Council, even if they only wanted to protect her. She deserved more than to be someone's job.

Through the taking of her blood, he'd seen her life, her fear and above all her strength. She was terrified.

He understood her terror and could relate. Yet even though she was afraid, there was also a part of her willing to stop, turn around and fight. He'd seen her love for Sophie and what she'd be willing to do for her friend. He'd also seen the way she thought of him and the kiss they'd shared.

William couldn't think about that. He needed to concentrate.

Katie was weak. He'd been surprised at how quickly he'd managed to drain her and how much of his blood she'd needed to survive. Her magic was on the point of killing her. Not because she was a bad witch, but because she'd been trying to suppress her powers. William hadn't told her yet that in order to sustain a healthy balance she had no choice but to use the powers gifted to her. Why was it that witches like Katie always got the fucked-up end of the scale?

He crouched down, watching the dark circles under her eyes disappear.

Her refusal to use her magic, to understand where it came from, was killing her. Gently — he didn't want to wake her too soon — he trailed a finger across her cheek. So vulnerable. It was like Emma had come back to him.

He cursed, moving away from her. He took a huge gulp of whisky from the bottle. He would do anything to numb these feelings.

He glanced down at his watch again. She'd been under for almost twenty-four hours. But it was working. He could see the colour returning to her skin and her body beginning to awaken of its own accord. Sometimes, after a forced blood feed like he'd done, the body could not sustain itself and would need reawakening before the bond could begin. With Katie being a witch, it helped to speed up the process. What didn't help was how weak she had been to start off with, but all was well. She was waking up.

"Come on, sweet cheeks." He looked at the time. "I haven't got all day." As he got older he'd found that he didn't need as much sleep, so his days were longer. He'd spent all morning watching her for any sign that she was reviving. Watching her and wanting. Katie wasn't like any other female he'd met, not because of her magic but because of what she'd gone through. She'd experienced loss.

These morbid thoughts would be the death of him.

He was pleased he hadn't killed her. Taking just enough blood had never been his strong point.

Her groan made him look at her face again.

Her eyes were open but she'd raised a hand to her temple.

Should he tell her he'd had to knock her out to stop the fire erupting from her hands? On second thoughts, he could keep information like that to himself.

She rolled over, coming to her knees.

"What happened?" She got to her feet but missed her footing and nearly fell flat on her face.

William caught her. "I've got you, little one." He spoke to try to calm and soothe her.

Her head shot up as soon as he spoke.

"You bloody bit me." She raised her hand to her neck to inspect the damage. A good thing she'd been out for the count. Her neck was healed even though his feeding hadn't been clean. Usually women flocked to him and he could take whatever he wanted. Katie had been the first person he'd taken by surprise. Her blood had tasted pure, but with the hint of sunshine.

"I only took a little blood," he lied.

"It bloody hurt."

She tried to move away but he could see that she was dizzy.

"Tell you what, darling—you rest on me while I get us to the car." He began escorting her out of his house.

"Whose dress is this?"

The question startled him. "My sister's."

He helped her into the car, not bothering looking at her, then started the car up and they were on their way to the Vampire Council.

"How did I get it on?" she queried.

He smirked. "I put it on for you."

Her gasp forced him to stop the chuckle erupting from his mouth. His little witch was such a prude.

"You've seen me naked," she shrieked, making him wince. He was sure the sound had perforated his ear drum.

"I've seen a lot of women naked."

He pushed down on the accelerator. Yes, he'd seen a lot of women naked, but none of them with the alluring purity that she projected. William was pleased the only thing he'd done was dress her. He'd been many things in his life, but a rapist wasn't one of them.

"You'd never seen *me* naked before."

"Well I can scrub it off my list of women to see. May I also say the beauty spot on your hip is quite eye catching? I struggled to dress you at all. From the sweet honey smell coming from you, I'd say no man has ever seen you naked before. I'm privileged. Women in this generation have many lovers by your age."

He heard her growl of mortification but he couldn't help but smile. He only spoke the truth. She was a beautiful creature and the sooner she got her powers under control the sooner she'd be able to grow and blossom. At the moment she was a shell, an empty vessel on the point of dying. He rubbed his chest, not liking the thought of her death.

He could smell the blood flooding her cheeks. The poor woman was embarrassed. He would have to remember how innocent she was.

"When will I see Sophie?" she asked.

She wasn't going to like the answer.

"You'll see her at the Council but you won't be allowed to speak to one another." He stopped the car outside the house where the Council would be meeting.

He tensed, sniffing the air. No...it couldn't be. He looked around but he couldn't see any signs.

"Why not?" she said, interrupting his searching.

He shook his head. It must be all the alcohol he'd been drinking. Shrugging his shoulders, he got out of the car.

"Showtime."

"Why not?" she asked again.

"You're being accused of withholding evidence. In vampire law, that is a serious offence. If you want my advice, stand, listen and keep your mouth shut."

"I can't do this," Katie said, fear striking inside her as she glanced at the dominating building.

"You've got no choice. You and Sophie should have trusted us." William made to grab her, but she pulled away, her hands going up to ward him off. "Don't even think about using your powers on me," he warned.

"Let me go," she pleaded.

William growled. Katie was begging him to let her go and, in his heart, all he wanted to do was let her run. The Council were not a friendly bunch and if they weren't careful Katie wouldn't be seen again. William hated the unfairness of their laws. It was one of the reasons he'd spent so long away from all that shit.

"I can't do it. I promised Robert I'd get you here safely, and that's why we started the blood—" He stopped, cursing his own stupidity.

"Started what?"

"We started the small base of the blood ceremony. I drained you and you drank my blood. It's why you feel revived. I fed you and we've started the connection. Look past your fear and you'll sense it, as clear as daylight."

William watched her hand go to her throat, where he'd bitten down. The bite marks were still prominent but the bruising had lessened in the few hours they'd been alone.

"How could you do this to me?"

The pain in her words tightened his gut, the connection between them stronger than he'd anticipated.

"I did it to save your life, and after this meeting, if you're still feeling pissed and on your high horse I'll give you permission to blow me up. Or—with your control—at least to try."

Katie nodded and William cursed as she started to run. He hated it when they ran.

"For fuck's sake, you crazy bitch. I promise to keep you safe," he yelled. Her little escape attempt was pathetic, and he caught her within seconds of her running.

"Never go up against a vampire when you're already weak."

He grabbed her roughly by the elbow, slammed the car door and escorted her indoors.

Chapter Nine

Sophie stood before the Council, just as she had three years ago. They all seemed older and more tired. Robert stood at her back, his hand on her waist reassuring her of his presence.

"I'm hearing some disturbing news, Robert, son of mine."

Robert turned to his father, showing him the respect he deserved. "What news would that be, Father?"

Sophie glanced at the disapproval on the faces of each of the men.

"This is ridiculous. How dare you come to the Council and pretend not to know the crimes this human has committed?" another councillor interrupted.

Sophie bowed her head, shamed and mortified that she had put Robert through this.

"Enough, Cedric." His father rubbed his hands over his eyes, clearly tired of it all. "What do you have to say, girl?"

Sophie was about to answer when a commotion interrupted her chain of thought.

"Let go of me, you disgusting brute." Katie came into the room, being pulled by a man who looked like Robert. Everything else about the man was completely different. His presence did not provoke the same respect that Robert's did, and he also appeared half crazy.

He took her to stand on the dais in front of the Council. As soon as he released her, Katie lashed out, striking William with an open-palmed slap.

He didn't move a muscle but immediately a hand print was visible on his skin. Sophie winced, pleased it wasn't her face.

William growled. He grabbed Katie's wrists and yanked them behind her, holding them in one hand and placing his other palm over her mouth, attempting to silence her. Sophie tried to go to her friend but Robert stopped her, his bruising grip warning her not to move.

"Who is this?"

"The witch, Father," William shouted for all to hear.

The Council erupted.

"How dare you try to fool us?"

"Is this some attempt to keep us from punishing the girl?"

"Blasphemy, I tell you!"

"Silence!" Robert's father yelled to the entire Council. "Who is this woman, William?"

"She is, indeed, a witch. I've got a wrecked house to prove it. She is also the named female under the protection of the blood bond between Robert, my brother, and his mate, Sophie Ford."

Sophie watched as he whispered something into Katie's ear, then slowly let her go. Katie glared at him, smiled at Sophie, then faced the Council.

This had been the first time in years Sophie had seen her friend's true spirit. She couldn't help but smile. What had happened to her? She looked fantastic.

"The blood bond between the mentioned parties hasn't been completed. So she is not under anyone's protection."

"Actually, Councillor Cedric, the bond is complete and the protection true and in place. I cannot allow any harm to come to either woman by our own bonded laws." Robert spoke clear and true.

The fuss began to build again.

"Are you saying you'll go against the Council's word?" one of them asked.

"By the Council's own laws, I have no choice. *You* have a choice." Robert saw that he had gained their attention. "You have a choice. Over there stands a woman, a first-generation witch. It has been centuries since the apparent extermination of their kind, but somehow one family survived. There may be more, but for now she is our one key to protecting our race, and the humans, from the annihilation and the corruption of the wolves. They are growing stronger by the second. You kill her, you kill our chances of balance and survival."

Robert was convincing. Sophie could feel the panic growing in her stomach.

"What of the girl?"

Robert glanced down at her and Sophie felt her heart melt under his searching gaze. "Without this girl, this woman—my mate—Katie wouldn't have been brought to us. Everything they've done, they've done to protect each other. I don't believe they should be punished. I think they should be congratulated."

"Your thoughts will be taken into account."

"I'd like to add a few words," William interrupted.

Sophie was shocked to see how many Council members seemed to dislike him. William began without their permission.

"Already, the wolves have attacked. I don't know if they intended to kill or capture Katie, but they know who and what she is. Surely we must protect her?"

The Councillors nodded, reluctantly taking on board what he had to say.

"We'll conduct this meeting and get back to you," Robert senior said. The Councillors started to move out.

Sophie turned to Robert, throwing her arms around him.

Everything was going to be all right.

Somewhere, glass smashed. Growls and screams erupted inside the house.

Robert tensed. "Attack! We're under attack."

Gunshots fired. The very ground beneath her feet began to shake.

Wolves crashed through the main hall, going straight for the Council. Sophie watched as Katie reacted, her hands shooting out and blowing up one of the wolves before going for the next. Another and another came in. The commotion was loud, fast and horrific. Many of the Councillors were slaughtered where they stood before they had time to react. So much carnage between two races.

Everywhere she looked, she saw destruction.

Robert sheltered her behind his broad back, but no matter what he tried he couldn't keep her from seeing.

When some of the bodies hit the floor, they took on human form. Sophie whimpered. This was too much. They were supposed to be protected here. This was vampire ground.

What was she supposed to do? They were everywhere. She was the only mortal being in the building.

She felt so helpless as she watched death unfold.

Robert felt Sophie's fear and he lashed out. Everything he could get his hands on, he took out. He kept Sophie at his back. He couldn't do anything more than protect her. William was helping Katie, but Robert could already see her power draining away. It was like all the life was being zapped out of her. The colour was disappearing from her cheeks. Her body looking more and more frail and brittle, like a zombie.

He knew she hadn't harnessed her power before and if she kept using it now she would be killed.

She shot out one last bolt and collapsed to her knees, a few droplets of blood escaping her lips as she clutched her chest.

Sophie screamed her name even as William was at her side, trying to move her.

They were out of time.

"Enough!" a voice filled with authority yelled at the room. The clapping of hands stopped everyone from moving. The wolves stopped, too, waiting for more orders.

Robert turned towards the voice. A voice from his past.

James, the Alpha of the wolves in Beyer West, stood in the doorway.

"Wow, that was really easy," he laughed. He looked a little insane.

Robert held Sophie to him. No matter what happened, he needed to keep her safe.

James swatted away the guard approaching him. Robert couldn't believe the power the man possessed. He walked straight across the room to where his father stood. Robert tried to move his feet, but he couldn't. Protecting his father was important but he couldn't move. He looked over at William and saw that he had the same problem. What was stopping them from moving?

The only being with that kind of magic was a witch. The only witch they knew of was collapsed in this room. What was going on?

"So, you're the main man causing me problems. You know this place is considered a deep, dark palace or a shrine to all the dead-walking vampires. Very few people will go past the doors to enter and be within these walls. I've never believed in the true power of the vampires and I've just proven to more people besides the wolves that your magic is not what it's supposed to be." James circled Robert's father.

Robert wanted to scream, to run, but his voice wouldn't work.

"What do you want from us?" his father growled.

James chuckled. "I want you all dead." He began laughing. "But I'll settle for just you."

Claws shot from his fingers and he severed the older man's throat. Robert tried to scream, and he saw William's mouth open in a cry, but no sound came from their mouths. He'd just watched his father be killed and he could do nothing.

James set fire to the body and whistled as he moved away. "Wow, that was easy," he said again.

A ball of rage grew inside Robert.

James went over to where Katie knelt, spent, on her knees. She coughed and blood spurted onto the ground. White formed in the tips of her hair. Sophie was yelling for Katie to get up. Robert could see her shaking.

"My little dove. It's time for us to go."

"N—no," she cried out weakly.

Putting his hand beneath her chin, he pulled her to her feet. Katie didn't have the energy to fight.

"You're mine and I'm taking you with me," James growled in her face.

"William," she screamed as James went to pick her up. She batted his hands away.

Robert watched his brother fighting to get to the witch.

"Let her go, dog."

James glanced at William and Robert in turn. "You didn't really think I'd allow my daughter to spend time with you, did you?"

The confession sent a shock wave through the room. Never before had a wolf and a witch mated and created a baby. It was unheard of. Yet, it explained everything—her anger, her weakness and how she was able to blow up wolves.

James picked Katie up and walked out of the room, leaving chaos and destruction in his wake.

Robert watched William fight. His brother couldn't move and watching her in their enemy's arms was killing him.

It was over an hour before Robert could move again. His father's body was nothing but ash, the Council defeated and left reeling. William looked angry and lost. As the magic levels dropped, Robert charged over to his father's body while William ran out into the street.

There was nothing he could do.

He went outside to join William. Sophie stood next to him staring up and down the street. There was no sign of where they could have gone.

"Did you know?" William turned on Sophie.

"Did I know what?" she asked, tears streaming down her face.

"Did you know your little witch friend was a descendent of a wolf?" he yelled at her.

Sophie hugged her arms around her body. "Up until a couple of hours ago I didn't even know wolves existed! How the hell could I have known she was one?"

Robert heard the grief in her voice and it was cutting him up. He grabbed her, protecting her with his body and his love.

"That's enough, William," Robert ordered. "You need to think clearly. There is no way that Katie could be any relation to James."

"How can you be so sure?" Robert watched as William wiped the tears from his eyes.

"Balance. Nature may be defiant but it still works on the balance of natural forces." Robert was certain of it.

"Fuck the balance. Did you just see what that prick did?" William pushed his brother away in his rage.

"I was there. I watched him and I couldn't move. Our father is dead and now everyone is going to turn to me for leadership." Robert poked William's chest, emphasising his point.

William began to laugh. "You've been waiting your whole life for this. What are you going to tell Mother? Our family, everything we've been working towards...destroyed."

Robert hadn't had time to process what had happened or to decide what he would have to tell his mother and siblings. It still hadn't really registered that his father was dead. In this world there would be no justice for the killing of a vampire. The humans didn't know that werewolves existed, let alone that they lived among them.

"He was too strong. No werewolf has that amount of power."

"Unless he has a witch protecting him." William confirmed what Robert was thinking.

"We need to find the witch and stop them."

Robert shook his head. "Katie can wait. I've got other, more importan—"

William turned on him in an instant.

"We have *nothing* more important. James's witch is going to help him whether we like it or not. We don't even know who his witch *is*. Katie is my top priority."

"We'll find her."

William refused to listen. "I promised to keep her safe. I won't stop until I find her. *I'll* be the one to find her. I screwed up—me."

He moved away, limping through the debris left behind by the wolves invading the Council. To most it would look like a raid gone bad, but to Robert it signalled the start of the chaos he knew was about to begin.

Robert watched his brother go. What was he supposed to do? He gazed back at the broken building where the Council had resided. This would break his mother. How was he supposed to take over from his father when he had no idea what he was supposed to do himself?

Sophie touched his back. He felt her heart open up to him. He welcomed her affection. It was the only thing keeping him going. She hugged him. The comfort reassured him.

"We have to go back inside."

Sophie nodded, placing her hand in his as he led the way back inside. They walked around the fallen bodies of his brethren.

The remaining members of the Council were gathered around his father's fallen body.

"He was a good man. A good leader. He didn't deserve to go like this."

They all murmured their agreement.

Robert stood before them. "I'll get my people to come and move the body. A quick burial should be sufficient."

All the Councillors turned to him. He could see the grief and sorrow on their faces.

One of them spoke up. "You must take his place now, Robert."

Robert didn't look to see where the voice had come from. He didn't want to know.

"The time for Councils and meetings is past. Did you see how easily they got to us?" That voice belonged to a frightened guard—one of the few who had managed to remain alive.

"We should have killed the girl when we had the chance." Cedric spoke harshly.

Sophie gasped—it was clear his words hurt her.

Robert growled at him. Without his father, with the death of an empire that had just happened, he didn't care about protocol. This man didn't deserve his respect and he would no longer get it.

"I would keep your words in your mouth if I were you," Robert warned him. None of the other members came forward to defend him. He didn't care—he would fight them all.

"How dare you speak to me like that?" Cedric said, red, puffy and outraged.

"How dare I? *How dare I?*" Robert charged at the man and took him by the scruff of the neck. "For years I've done whatever the Council has told me to do. I've killed and I've worked with nothing but the Council's good name in mind. My father taught me that there is nothing better in this world than pleasing the Council for the good of mankind." He stopped and brought his face closer. "If we hadn't started those rumours, if we had worked for the good of everyone, Katie wouldn't have gone off the radar and she would have been safe and protected. A good man died today and a good, powerful witch was taken from us. I suggest you keep your tongue in your head before you start questioning people." He shoved the man away from him, turning to the other members.

"I think you should all go home. Spend time with your families and loved ones. The werewolves have just declared war. We have no choice but to fight back. Go home, rest, think about the future. And if you want a future without a threat from the wolves, then come back here and we'll rebuild."

Robert went back to Sophie, taking her by the hand.

"We've got to change. Otherwise, we won't exist anymore. They're coming for us whether we want them to or not and I refuse to go down without a fight."

Sophie was shaking uncontrollably. One by one they left, until only Sophie and Robert stood over the body of his father. She held his hand but remained silent. She obviously understood his need to think.

"You can leave if you want," he finally said.

Sophie glanced over at him, but his gaze stayed firmly on his father's remains.

She licked her lips. "I don't want to go."

He turned to her then.

"It's going to get ugly," he warned.

"I don't care. I have nowhere else to go," she admitted, tears streaming from her eyes. Katie was gone. Her parents wouldn't understand. The only people she had in the world were Katie and Robert. She didn't want to leave him.

He kissed the top of her head. "This is going to be dangerous."

Sophie shrugged her shoulders. "Life is never supposed to be easy."

"I have to tell my mother."

"I'll be there when you do. I promise, Robert, I will always be there for you."

She couldn't believe that she was about to meet her other family — Robert's family — and that she would be bringing them awful news. Sophie knew she'd met his mother back at the bonding ceremony, but she hadn't talked to her at all. This would be the first time they would meet properly, and when she should be taking round a cake and offering to make tea, she would instead be part of giving news of death. Not the best way to start with the in-laws.

Sophie thought of Katie. There was no way Katie was involved with or part of the wolves' plans.

She turned to Robert. This couldn't wait. "I met her parents. Katie's. Before they died. She looks so much like them. They were wonderful people, Robert. There is no way that man could be her father. No way her parents would ever deal with a man so evil," she earnestly pleaded.

Robert hugged her to his body, nodding his head. "He said it to cause a reaction. To make us doubt everything."

She circled her arms around him. She needed to know that he was alive and that everything was fine. She needed to reassure herself.

"I'm fine," he soothed, kissing the top of her head.

"I've never been so scared in all of my life. I saw them coming and I didn't know what to do," she confessed. She inhaled his scent, loving the feel of him under her skin. "I'm sorry about your father," she told him. Everything had happened so fast.

"I can't mourn him. I don't have time to mourn him." He looked into her eyes. "We'll find Katie, I promise."

She ducked her head. "I know we will. I just hope she's alive when we do."

He took her chin between his fingers. "Let's go see Mother, then get you home."

His mother broke down. She was inconsolable. The tears refused to stop. His two sisters stayed silent but comforted their mother. He could see the despair on all of their faces. Rose stared at him with desperation shining in her eyes. The youngest female of them all, and yet her eyes held a world of knowledge.

He went to her and kissed her on the forehead. "I'll take care of you. I promise."

"He shouldn't have died," she cried.

Dawn, his other sister, took her off his hands and all three women huddled together. Not able to cope with the loss in his heart at seeing his family broken, Robert turned away. He left Sophie with them while he and his other two brothers went into the study. William should have been here. Katie would be found and looked after, but William, as the next oldest brother, should be in this study with them, planning the next fight.

"We could have been there to help," said Jason, the youngest, cutting into Robert's thoughts. Out of all the brothers Jason was the most likely to strike first and ask questions later. The one to run into battles without a plan.

Robert placed a comforting hand on his arm. "It wouldn't have mattered. Father would have died anyway."

"I can't believe he's really dead," Adam whispered. The next brother after William. Adam was often silent, but when he spoke he made sense.

"I need you to be ready. We've got a war on our hands and, when the time comes, we'll need to strike back against them."

"What about this witch?" Jason asked.

Robert shook his head. "I believe William has connected himself with the witch. He's going to be doing nothing but trying to find her."

They fell silent, all of them thinking of Emma. The one person who had given William her heart, then taken it away. William, out of all of them, knew how to deal with loss, but he wouldn't come here.

"Who is the witch helping James?" Adam questioned.

Robert shook his head. "I've no idea. Without Katie, we're powerless against them. Attacks will increase now. They'll see the Valentines as weak. Not only the wolves, but others as well. They are strong, my brothers. Stronger than anything we're used to. If you see one of them, you must promise to run away."

He could tell he'd shocked them. Never before would he have allowed them to run. He hated giving the order. But he'd seen first-hand what they could do. He didn't want to risk any more of his family. The truth was, the Valentines weren't ready for a battle. If anything, the vampires had become complacent about their power. All of that was about to change.

They both nodded. All of them were scared, not knowing what the future held. Their father would have told them what to do and why they were doing it. But he was gone. They only had each other now.

"I noticed your bond mate," Jason said, changing the subject.

Robert smiled. Sophie was the only thing he had to smile about lately. "You must find a mate of your own."

"How does it feel?" Adam asked. They both seemed intrigued by the prospect of a bond mate. They had all heard stories of how wonderful it could be.

"It's wonderful." Robert smiled at his brother before going back to kiss his mother goodnight.

He took Sophie with him to his apartment above the club.

"Your mom seemed nice." Sophie spoke first to break the silence.

Robert went to her and kissed her on the lips, tasting her. "I don't want to talk. I want to forget about the past few hours. I just want to feel you in my arms. Do you understand?"

Sophie nodded.

Robert took her in his arms. "You're the only good thing about tonight. I couldn't bear losing you." He kissed her over and over again, making sure she was really there, in his apartment, in his arms.

"I'm here, Robert and I'm never leaving you." She responded to his kiss. She stripped off his shorts and scored her nails into his flesh. "Feel me. I'm here, with you." She laid loving kisses where her nails had raked the skin. She lavished attention on him.

"More, Sophie. I need more."

She smoothed her lips along his chest, her hands going to the buckle on his trousers. She pushed his trousers down past his ankles, stood up to kiss him. She lifted her arms so he could remove her dress. Sophie wore nothing underneath. Naked, they pressed against each other head to toe.

He cupped her ass, prompting her to jump and wrap her legs around his waist.

They didn't have time to get to the bedroom. Robert took her against the wall, positioning his hardened shaft at her entrance and plunging into her pussy, going right to the hilt. They both cried out at the contact, forgetting in that instant together about the troubles that lay ahead.

Robert and Sophie climbed the wall of fulfilment until they collapsed in each other's arms.

Chapter Ten

Sophie woke up wrapped in Robert's arms. Had it really been three days since she'd come back to him? How could her life have changed so much in such a short amount of time? She'd become his mate, the Council had been attacked and Katie had been kidnapped.

She was sad and angry, but her heart was happy. She was in love with this man.

Three years ago she'd been awoken by him, protected by him. Within seventy-two hours, he'd captured her heart and now he owned her.

"What are you thinking?" he asked, reaching for her as soon as he woke up.

"How much our lives have changed in three simple days." She stroked the arm lying across her naked belly. He was warm to the touch.

"Welcome to the world of vampires. Life moves a little too quickly sometimes."

She smiled. "I'm conflicted," she admitted.

"Why, my love?"

"Am I your love?" she asked.

"I've attached myself to you for eternity, Sophie."

She smiled.

She was going to tell him.

Taking a deep breath, she let the words roll off her tongue. "I love you."

Silence met her confession. She waited, tense, unsure.

He kissed her, stopping her from vocalising her thoughts. "I told you your mind would soon know what your body and heart knew already."

She laughed.

"I love you, too, my sweet Sophie."

Sophie rolled him onto his back, resting up on her arms. She smiled down at him.

"Everything is going to change now," she whispered, staring out at the starlit sky.

Sophie felt him sigh.

"Yes, I feel it is."

"I've only just found you and I feel like I'm going to lose you."

He tightened his hold on her. "I'll never leave you."

"Do you swear?"

"You have my word."

It wasn't enough, but for the moment it would have to do. Sophie snuggled close to him, relishing the comfort and warmth he supplied, knowing in her heart that something drastic was going to happen to change it all.

* * * *

William paced in his house, feeling as though he was losing his sanity. The whisky and brandy bottles lay at his feet, empty. This wasn't supposed to happen. He should have protected her. Found some way to save her. No matter what he thought, he could only come to the same conclusion—he was destined to fail every female he cared about. But he refused to give up. Katie needed him.

He had just stood there, unable to move while his worst enemy had taken another woman away from him. It was Emma all over again. He couldn't allow it to happen this time. He couldn't let her die, let history repeat itself. Katie wasn't dead and he wouldn't give up until he'd done everything he could to get her back.

Katie wasn't a werewolf. He knew it. So why did he feel there was something he was missing?

Where would they take her? His brain scrambled to figure out the answer.

He glanced down at her blood-soaked clothes. There was more at stake now. James, leader of the Beyer West pack, had just signed his own death warrant. William was now determined to be the one to end that fucking wolf's life if it was the last thing he did. First, he would find Katie and he'd make sure she still breathed before he went for the wolf.

They were connected by blood. William had to calm down. He must put all of his energy into opening the bridge he'd kept numb and closed off for centuries. Rubbing his hands together, he thought about what had happened the last time he'd opened it up. No, he couldn't think of Emma. Emma was dead, but Katie…she was still living.

Sitting in the centre of his living room, he focussed on everything he knew about Katie. Hair the colour of amber honey, soft to the touch. His knuckles tingled as he imagined the slide of her hair against his hand. Her eyes, wide and fearful but, when happy, filled with a feisty heat he craved. Her figure was petite from years of draining her resources, but he also saw a woman who would face any battle. She was strong and fiery, weak and brave. Vulnerable and alone.

The connection brightened like a spark. He felt her. He knew her.

She was travelling in a locked van, her eyes covered. He could feel her fear and it was choking him. Her hands were bound. She didn't know where she was.

William came out of the vision gasping for breath. It was too much. Katie might be physically weak but her mind was strong. Too strong. He was fearful. Her mind was strong like a light bulb shining the brightest just before it blows.

He needed to get to Katie, and fast.

If she used more magic it would consume her and Katie would fall, like many witches before her, into the pits of hell.

He got up from his place on the carpet and left his life and world behind, in search of the woman who could answer not only the world's prayers—but also his own.

Epilogue

"Let go of me," she begged, over and over again. No one answered. She was trapped in a room with nothing for company but the glass walls keeping her caged in. Her chest felt tight all the time. The room was too small, the air too thin.

They were treating her like an animal, giving her food in bowls. Horrible sludge she wouldn't even feed to a dog.

She hadn't showered in days and men kept coming and looking at her, like a pet in a zoo. She hated them. Their looks.

When she was alone, she tried to think of ways to escape, but she wasn't allowed out of this room.

The only time anyone spoke to her was when *he* came to the room.

"Hello, my princess."

He was softly spoken but he scared the living daylights out of her. He tried to get her to use her magic, but warning bells kept going off in her head. Using her magic didn't feel right.

"What do you want from me?" she screamed when he came to her with more needles and more tests.

Afterwards he would come back and try to soothe her. Katie was too exhausted to move, let alone flinch away from his touch.

She missed Sophie. She missed her parents' house. She prayed for hours for them to come and find her.

She missed William. The horrible vampire with the bad attitude. At least he had given her freedom.

Katie wanted to live. She didn't want this. She just wanted to be normal.

Finally, after another day of tests, she collapsed in a ball on the floor. *He* returned, moving into the room, and he looked happy.

"You're the one. The one I've been searching for, for so long." He knelt beside her and cupped her cheeks. They were dry from the lack of sun.

How long had she been stuck down here, anyway?

"I want to go home," she pleaded with him again.

He lifted her up off the dirt floor and carried her out of the room. Katie didn't know what to do or where to turn.

She just hoped with all her heart that William would find her before they killed her.

WILLIAM

Dedication

I would like to thank my family for all the love and support. Also, I would like to say a huge thank you to Rebecca Hill, my lovely editor. Without you this wouldn't be possible.

Prologue

A few hundred years ago

The sounds filling the air were of running feet and heavy, panicked breathing. Two people running for their very lives. They ran through the forest, not sure what was coming. William could feel the power coming towards them, not seeking to help their situation but to destroy them.

"Run, Emma." William grabbed her hand and urged her forward.

"I'm trying. I can't continue anymore," she gasped, slowing to a stop, grabbing her side in pain.

"We don't have time for this." He pulled on her arm and tried to get her to move, his fear for her life making him forget she was only human. She cried out, falling to her knees.

"Stop, William, please. I can't go on," she sobbed.

He glanced down and saw her agony. They'd been running for well over an hour. William looked through the thick layers of leaves and trees, nodding. He crouched down beside her.

"We can stay and rest a little." His eyes strayed to the trees all around them—any one of them could hide a foe.

She shook her head. "You should go on."

He disagreed. "I'm not losing you." He held her face—beautiful; this was the woman he had fallen in love with—and he could see how weak she was. Already, her face was beginning to look gaunt and shadows were appearing underneath her eyes. He knew in his heart of hearts that unless she rested she would not be able to make it.

He laid a gentle kiss on her lips. They felt dry even against the barest touch. He could taste death and he couldn't...he *wouldn't* accept it.

"We're in this together. No matter what." He held her against the strength of his body. "Take some more of my blood."

He made to bite into his flesh, to make it easier for her to drink the powerful liquid, but her hand on his arm stopped him.

"No, no more."

He nodded reluctantly, holding her cold body against him, humming to himself. He could even smell a change within her, almost an acceptance of what was about to happen. It terrified him. He kept looking around for any signs of danger, hoping and praying that he wouldn't find any. William wouldn't be able to protect them both for long. He wasn't strong enough.

William knew, deep down, that this sense of calm was about to end. His brother Robert had already told him what to expect. His father had shipped his mother, younger brothers and sisters off out of danger the moment it had all gone wrong. The witch hunts had grown more deadly than any of them could have imagined. A madman's accusations…and now this. Humans hunting them as though they were nothing but dogs, forcing them to run for their lives.

None of them were safe anymore.

"They're coming. I can feel them, William. So much anger and fear, and it's all for us." He could hear the fear in her voice. They had survived many attempts on their lives—they were immortal, after all. But never had anything scythed through their numbers so quickly. Just as a plague kills humans, now the humans were a plague to the immortals, killing them off one by one.

"Don't worry—just rest," he told her, but his eyes stayed on the forest. He could feel them there. He couldn't see them, but it wouldn't be long until they were here.

Just then, Emma started to panic in his arms, lashing out with her hands and screaming, 'Get off me, get off me', over and over again. He couldn't see what had her so terrified.

"Emma? What is it?" He was helpless. She was screaming and crying for him to help her and he didn't know how. There was nothing near her that could hurt her.

Laughter emerged from the tree line, followed by a male form.

"Witches are such pesky little things."

William stood and squared off against James, the Alpha wolf of the Beyer West pack.

"What are you doing here?" William asked.

A female followed him—her eyes were shut, James guiding her by the hand, and he could tell that she was chanting. William was confused. Why would Emma be terrified of what was coming when James was bringing reinforcements? James was one of them, he wouldn't attack them. Would he? But the wolves were supposed to be taking cover…

"Yes. My little witch, it seems, is more powerful than your witch."

James leant down to where Emma sat crying. "Boo."

William shoved the other man away. "Leave her alone."

They circled each other in hunting stances. The sounds around them were of the mystery witch chanting and Emma whimpering.

"What are you doing here? You're the leader of the wolves." They could live among the humans, which meant that they were safe and could help vampires and witches to hide from the search parties.

The wolves were in hiding…weren't they?

"Well, you see, here is my problem. I'm supposed to risk my neck, and those of my wolves…for what, exactly? For you and your vampires? You see, I suddenly had this idea." William had a sick feeling in his gut as he listened to James talk. "This idea of what would happen if the witches and vampires who controlled me and told me what to do just disappeared…poof. Then I suddenly wondered what would happen if I screamed devil and witch in a room full of humans. You see, William Valentine, the mind is a dangerous thing. They went nuts." James started to laugh, the sound hysterical.

He was mad—barking mad. William couldn't grasp what he was telling him. He refused to believe it.

But looking into James' eyes, he knew.

"You led the humans right to us."

All this time their father had wondered how so many witches and so many of their own kind could have been hunted and killed within just months. Now it seemed obvious. Someone had to have known—someone from the inside.

The leader of the Beyer West Pack, one of the most powerful werewolves in the world, had destroyed hundreds of witches and vampires alike.

"Yes!" James jumped up and down with joy. A rather strange and child-like thing to do.

William felt like he was going to throw up. All this time, the person they had believed was helping them had been the one destroying their kind.

"But the one downside is that I have to have a witch of my own. Helps to weaken yours. You should be thankful—she's the one sending the humans off in the other direction at the moment. We're safe for now." James patted the chanting witch on the shoulder. "You can stop now, my dear."

"So how shall we spend our time together?" James asked William.

William saw the hundreds of dead faces. Remembered the reports of a vampire being burnt in the sunlight, of witches being hunted and killed. Months of agony, trying to protect his friends.

William was still a young vampire. He couldn't control himself. He lashed out and dived for James, going for the other man's throat. James swatted him down as if he were no more than a bug. William got up and went for him again, landed a punch that knocked James to the ground. He fought fiercely but there was no way he could win. James was the leader of an entire race; William, the younger son of the most powerful vampire. His older brother Robert might be able take James, but not him. He never stood a chance.

As William charged at him one final time, James had obviously already seen his opportunity. He grabbed William around the neck and pinned him to the ground, standing over him, his foot resting heavily on his chest.

William was stuck. He couldn't move.

"You know, I came here to see if you'd join me. I've heard about you. You never do as you're told. A free spirit. The one Daddy Vamp can't control. Join me, William, and together we could own this world."

William hated the power his family had and he'd never wanted to be part of that world. But as much as he pissed his father off, he still loved him — he was still his father.

"Never," he growled, blood landing on James's face.

James wiped the blood away with the material of his shirt. "Big mistake."

James tightened his hold on William's neck. The pressure felt as though James was going to rip his head from his body…which was one of the few things that would kill him.

William closed his eyes, praying for Emma.

"Big mistake, wolf." A flash of light threw James off him. Emma was standing, pale and shaking, her hair dishevelled.

James collapsed in a heap across from William, but he wasn't dead.

"The next time you get a little witch, get one who knows how to do a chant properly," Emma panted. A burst of flames consumed the other witch as Emma was hit by the final blast from the other witch.

William could feel Emma's pain, but the other witch *screamed*.

"Nooo!" James yelled. "Bitch!"

Emma threw more magic his way. William grabbed her before she allowed it to consume them both. She had created enough of a diversion.

They ran.

Neither of them was powerful enough to take down James and William needed to get to his father. He needed to warn everyone.

How was he going to tell his father — their leader — that they were at war with the wolves?

"William, stop." He stopped and turned to the love of his life, then gasped.

She looked old; her hair was grey and her face gaunt.

"We have to go," he insisted. "You're using too much magic."

She paused and pressed a kiss to his palm. "*You have to go. You must tell your father.*"

"Together, we can do this together," he earnestly pleaded.

She shook her head. "I love you, William, and that's why I have to help you. He will keep coming. James won't stop."

"Don't do this," he begged, tears falling from his eyes.

"I love you, Will. I always have. Listen to me. You will find another."

He shook his head in denial.

"You will. I've seen it. You love me but you're not meant for me. You're meant for another." She rested his palm against her heart. He could feel the steady beat. She wasn't afraid — she had accepted her fate.

Once a witch knew what she had to do, in the steady beat of her heart, there was no stopping it.

William looked into the face of the woman he had loved for more than a century. She was his bonded mate. He loved her with all his heart and soul. He couldn't imagine life without her.

She kissed him one final time.

"Well, isn't this a touching scene?" James was standing a few feet away.

William broke the kiss and stared into the face of the man he was going to hunt for the rest of his life.

"You interrupted us." Emma turned to him.

William noted the squared shoulders, the jaw set with determination. She was here for business and she was taking James with her.

"You killed my witch," he growled.

"You killed hundreds of mine." He could hear the anger and the rage. Her kind—her race. She was fighting for them. For the countless men and women who had lost their lives in this man's hunt for domination.

"Well, that was just plain fun," James gloated.

Emma screamed and threw all her power against him. It was awful to see. William watched and could do nothing. She'd cast a spell to keep him in place. He could only watch James winning, taunting her with his own abilities.

Finally she threw enough power against him, using up the last of her magic in a killing blow. James disappeared.

She collapsed in a bloodied heap on the ground.

William felt the magic wear off, releasing him, and he ran to her side.

The tears rolled down his cheeks, thick and fast.

"Oh God, Emma." He cradled her so that she was draped across his lap.

Her face was pale, blood spilling from her mouth. "Go and warn the others."

"I love you," he said.

It was too late. She was gone.

William held her to him for the longest time. Her pale, lifeless body in his arms, laid against his heart.

Time passed. It didn't matter. He held her and he felt nothing.

"William... William... William..." He heard his name spoken, but he didn't care.

Eventually he looked up to see his brothers, Robert, and Adam. They were waiting for him.

"I couldn't save her," he cried.

"Come with us." Robert held out his hand.

He shook his head. He couldn't leave her—he and Emma were meant to be together.

Adam shoved Robert out of the way and growled at William. "Look, William, it won't help the situation if you just stay here and die."

Reluctantly, William let her go. A witch needed to be given back to the earth. It was their way. He couldn't take her with him. He laid her to rest, said his prayers and walked away with his brothers, a changed man.

Several hours later

James stood over the body of the dead witch. A waste, but worth it.

He moved over to the other witch and looked down into her face. She was a rare beauty. Her brown hair was tinted with the white of a witch who had abused her power.

"You should learn balance," he tutted.

He knelt by her side and touched her cold cheek. He stroked the cold, lifeless flesh, so still and silent in death.

He pulled back, laughing as Emma came to, choking and gasping for air. She pulled the air into her lungs as if it were a rare find.

"Had me worried there, little Em. Didn't think you were going to wake up." He handed her a cloak to cover her bloodied body.

She took it. He could see her fingers trembling.

"Spell go wrong?"

Once she'd placed the cloak around her shoulders, she got to her feet. She flipped her hair over one shoulder. "Spell went perfectly, didn't you think?" She placed her hand on her hip.

She was saucy and hot, and he'd come to appreciate her over these past months.

"It sure had William convinced," he agreed.

She didn't even bat an eyelash.

"Not concerned that your one and only mate thinks you're dead and innocent?" James asked.

She shrugged her shoulders. "You gave him the chance to join us; he wanted to stay with his daddy. That's his business. I'm not prepared to go back."

"Did you honestly think he'd join me—us?" James leaned against the tree, taking her in.

"He doesn't agree with his father. I guess he just thinks he's bad."

James hadn't been able to believe it when he'd got a visit from this witch, some months ago, late at night. She had wanted to join forces. She'd known it had been him who had started the hunts of the witches and vampires. Emma was an evil witch to the core and she was tired of being the good girl.

There was no love and no compassion in this package—just pure hatred.

The partnership worked very well.

"Remember what you promised me?" He walked over to her, his power and energy clashing with hers, sending tingles of pain shooting along his nerve endings.

"Yes, I know what I promised." She took a step back. A huge mistake. His wolf liked to see her scared. He could smell her fear.

"You'd better not mess with me, witch," he warned.

"I came to you, remember? No messing from my end. You'll get what you want and I'll get what I want." Her tone was insolent.

He didn't like it.

Within seconds he had wrapped his hand around her neck and was squeezing. "I want you to remember, sweet Emma, I don't care about you. I'm not William Valentine. You're one witch in a sea of others and any time I want I can pluck the next one out. You get on my nerves and your days are numbered." He thrust her away and turned from her.

"It's because of *her*, isn't it?" Emma cried.

He stopped, stood rigid and turned with a snarl on his face.

"You're doing this because—"

"I suggest that if you like breathing you keep your mouth shut."

He didn't speak again. He didn't need to. His warning was clear.

Chapter One

Present day

The sound of glass smashing could be heard in every corner of the bar. The audience looked on at the spectacle in silence, each doubtless wondering if they would be the target of the vampire's wrath.

"Where is she?" A fist was raised. Usually, bar fights were great sport, but in a predominantly vampire-filled bar there was no sport, just information gathering—and it wasn't acquired over tea and biscuits. It always got bloody and it never ended well. A Valentine was on the prowl and no one was about to get in his way—even if the vampire William targeted was scared for his life.

The way the other customers saw it, the guy getting pummelled shouldn't have earned a reputation for being a messenger to the wolves. A man supporting both sides of the war.

"I don't know, man. No one has talked." The guy covered his face, denying all knowledge. Adam stood and observed from the dark corner as he watched his older brother lose control. William was completely out of it.

Since another witch had been taken—Katie, the best friend of his brother Robert's bonded mate—it was like he was losing his sense of reality. No one could reason with him.

"Tell me where they are," William snarled in the young vampire's face. Adam winced. He was here as a favour to Robert and he loved his brother, but this was too damn much. There was no thought, no consideration of the chaos he was causing. It had hit him worse even than losing Emma. It was like someone had carved out his heart and left him hurt and bleeding.

Katie White, the last remaining witch, was still alive, and that made it worse. At least Emma had been dead and he'd known there was nothing he could do to change that. But William knew that Katie was out there, and he was leaving a wave of destruction everywhere he went in his efforts to find her.

William wasn't the same man. There was no mercy in this guy. Rage, anger and pain consumed him now. His was on a destructive path. No one—not even Robert—could stop him now.

Adam looked around at all the people observing the fight. Vampires, wolves...shit, even demons sat and watched William. Most of them looked terrified of the vampire who had clearly lost his mind.

Shaking his head, Adam turned back to watch his brother.

As much as he thought that this was wrong, he would never get in between his brother and what he felt he needed to do. The witch clearly meant something to him. No vampire went this crazy for a woman unless she was a bond mate.

Adam didn't know much about her. He'd never met her. A few months ago, she had been taken by the wolf Alpha, James. The same night his own father—head of the vampire council and the most powerful vampire in all of Beyer West—had been killed. Murdered, actually. Taken from them by the same wolf.

Everything around them was going to shit and his brother was determined to go down the same path. At any time the other customers could jump them and finally be rid of the unstable Valentine boy. For decades, William had made himself a reputation for being the crazy brother, but now he was driving his ruthlessness to a whole new level.

Adam tensed as the barman approached his brother. The barman was a vampire and, from the look of it, one of the older generation. Adam moved closer. If it went the wrong way he would back his brother. Whether he believed what his brother was doing was right or not, family came first.

That was what made him a Valentine.

Adam watched as William raised his fist, ready to take another set of swipes at the guy he held. The barman stopped his raised fist easily, holding it in his, and span William around as if he were nothing more than a rag doll.

"Son, he said he didn't know nothing. Leave him be," the barman said.

William hissed and tried to hit the barman, a great insult amongst their community. Out of respect, no one attacked the older generation. Adam swore and moved forward.

The barman grabbed William and, using the full force of his upper body, threw him against the bar. The bottles rattled and the customers close by dispersed, not wanting to get involved in a fight that was clearly about to get worse.

Adam ran, going for the man who was holding his brother. The barman turned and sucker-punched him across the room before Adam could even land a blow. He crashed through the window, broken shards of glass spraying around him.

"Fuck," Adam cursed. The only humans in the street were ones who had seen too much of this world and were pretty much crazy. Drunks, druggies and prostitutes who knew better than to talk about what they had seen. His fangs protruded as his anger rose.

Fuck protocol. Adam was pissed off and cruising for a fight.

He stormed back into the bar.

William was bloodied but he was getting in a few punches of his own.

"I've told you not to bring shit like this to my bar. I didn't serve your fucking family to have you ruin my business," the barman yelled as he pushed William away from him.

Adam stopped as his words registered. This man used to serve the Valentines?

"What the hell are you talking about?" William asked, spitting blood on the floor and wiping his lip.

"Name's Donald. I served the Valentines for over three generations and this is the type of respect I get?"

William pulled himself up off the floor.

Adam couldn't believe what his brother had done. Fucking asshole. Donald 'Don' Hargreaves was a well-known guard and warrior. He had fought for and protected the Valentines up until their youngest sister, Rose, had been born. After Rose had come home safe and sound, their mother healthy, Don had been relieved of his duties by their father. No explanations—nothing. Centuries had passed since this fierce warrior had been seen, which was why William hadn't recognised him. He'd done nothing other than working in a bar, where no one would have thought to look for him.

"Don Hargreaves?" Adam asked.

"Yep, that's me. About time you two heathens bloody noticed," Don replied, his anger still close to the surface.

"Shit." William wiped his face, smearing the blood along his cheek. "I'm sorry, Don. This had nothing to do with you."

"It has something to do with your father's death a few months back?" Don asked William.

"Part of it," replied Adam, who could see how much William was struggling to keep himself together. The natural instinct to hunt and kill was close to the surface, ready to erupt.

Don didn't look at Adam. He kept his eyes firmly on the other Valentine brother. The one whom he considered a threat, Adam supposed.

"What is all this about?" Don folded his arms.

Adam stared at William. After all, this was William's deal and he had nothing to do with it. He refused to talk about something he had no hand in.

"A witch was found a couple of weeks back." William raised his voice so that everyone in the room could hear.

Murmurs and gasps filled the room.

"Bullshit. Witches have all been killed off," one of the customers yelled.

Pretty much his first thought when he'd been told. Every vampire with a few years on them would remember the slaughter of the witches.

"Yeah, this is some shit you Valentines are selling. No witches. It's why the world has gone to shit," another agreed.

Growls and curses rang through the bar, all in agreement. There were no more witches.

Don cut them off by raising his hand. Silence came instantly. All of them were happy to shout and curse at the Valentines, but for Don, they shut up.

"This shit real?" Don asked.

"More real than you could ever imagine. I had her in my arms. I saw the power she's got. What she's capable of," William confirmed, his sincerity and adoration obvious to everyone.

Adam saw Don nod and look at each customer in turn, assessing the room.

"Who took her?" Don finally asked after a pause. A simple question, but all the immortals in the room looked at each other for the answer.

"The Alpha wolf, James. The same night he murdered my father," William replied.

"Shit," Don cursed.

Adam didn't have a clue what the older man was swearing at.

"What has the witch got to do with you?" the older man asked.

"I promised to take care of her," William answered.

"I swear we don't know anything here. This is a place for us all to come, relax and drink," Don told the Valentine men.

Adam looked around at the clientele again. They were all nodding. He wondered what the hell William was going to do. The man was on the edge. There was no predicting him anymore.

William glared around the room. Tonight had turned into another dead end, more useless information that led him nowhere. Not only had it led him nowhere, but straight into a fight with Don Hargreaves, the warrior who had supported his father back in the day, helping to support the alliance between the species. Back when they hadn't fought each other but had worked to protect each other and to build peace.

It seemed that Don had succeeded where their father had failed. His bar offered a place of safety for any immortal, with the promise that they would be protected by the warrior himself.

Wiping his brow, he felt the blood dripping down his face. He welcomed the rush of pain, the first real feeling he'd had since Katie had been taken from him.

"Any information you get, let me know?" William asked.

Don hesitated for a split second, then nodded. Satisfied with his answer, William turned to the room at large.

"I don't believe all of you are as innocent as you claim. Let the word on the street spread. Tell James, Alpha of the Beyer West Pack, that William Valentine is looking for him and he wants blood. I'm bringing this war to his door. That witch dies and his pack is forfeit."

William made sure his message was clear to all. They looked like a combination of scared and pissed off civilians. Quite frankly, he didn't give a fuck—he was on a mission and anyone who stepped in his way was about to have their life turned upside down.

"See you around," he said to Don, moving towards the door.

"How's your mother?"

The question took him by surprise. Turning around, he saw Don had shut down, a neutral expression firmly in place.

"She's coping as best she can." At least, that was what Adam had told him earlier.

"Send my regards."

William acknowledged Don, nodding one last time before leaving the bar.

Flicking open his phone, William placed a call. The phone rang and rang and, finally, on the last ring, someone picked up.

"You gave me wrong information. I'm coming for you." He flipped the phone closed and started walking away. Humans moved out of his way. They must be able to see the evil within. It was just beneath the surface, like a second skin.

Adam caught up with him and walked beside him, emanating anger.

William kept walking, steering them down an abandoned side street, the only place nearby suitable for a stand-off. Younger brother or not, William was on a mission and he intended to complete it.

"Why are you here?" he asked.

Adam shrugged.

Irritated, William repeated himself. He didn't like his questions to go unanswered.

"Robert sent me. He wants you home," Adam admitted.

William laughed, sounding hysterical. "And Robert thinks you're the one to do it," he mocked.

William didn't know why he was intent on hurting Adam, but he wanted him away from him. He no longer felt safe to be around. William could feel the beast rising inside him with every passing second that

Katie was away from him. If he wasn't careful, William knew he would hurt Adam.

His sense of her had melted when James had taken her. The only way Katie could be this invisible to him was if she was protected by a spell. Impossible, as Katie was the only known witch. But James had done *something* to keep her emotions, their connection, locked away.

"Robert is a little busy at the moment," Adam growled in reply. William turned back at his brother's words. William frowned, wondering what he'd said.

Several seconds later, he realised.

That's it, little brother, be angry with me. I can deal with anger.

"I'm sure having his little mate Sophie waiting in the wings to take care of his problems and dealing with being head of the council is really busy work." The sarcasm leaked from his tone.

His taunting was having the effect he desired. Adam's hand was fisted at his side. He looked ready to pounce. William needed to give him a little more ammunition to fuel the anger. He wanted to get rid of his brother and, by showing him his lack of caring, hopefully Adam would lose interest.

"Don't diss Sophie. She's been fantastic throughout all this. Which you'd see if you came home."

William didn't doubt it. She might be small but she was one tough gal, just like his Katie.

"Well I've got stuff to do—"

"What? Your crusade of trying to get yourself killed? Do you think Mum needs to deal with your little martyr complex?" Adam growled at him.

William tensed. His brother had no idea what was going on. Saving Katie was more than a martyr complex. He'd begun the mating ritual that distant night, long ago. She owned his heart and soul and he wouldn't rest until she lay safe and protected in his arms.

"Go back to Robert and give him your report." William dismissed him.

"Always the coward's way out," Adam hissed at his retreating back.

William reacted, spinning around and slamming Adam against the opposite wall. The brick building shifted. Any more pressure on the building and it would fall to the ground around their ears.

"What the fuck are you saying?" William's fangs sprang out, his aggression ready to find a target.

"You're nothing but a coward," Adam yelled the words at him, pressing against the arms that held him against the shaking building.

"You'd better be thankful you're my brother—"

"Or what?" Adam interrupted him.

William was tempted to hit him, but as soon as the thought came to him he dropped his arms. He would never—could never—hurt his brothers or sisters. A small amount of control was coming back to him. Where moments ago he'd wanted to hurt his brother—to do damage—the idea now repulsed him. An image of Katie smiling at him broke into his mind, fracturing him into a million pieces. She would be ashamed of him if she saw William attacking his own brother.

William sagged and let Adam go, the shame of what he'd been about to do to his brother filling him with utter regret.

"Come home," Adam pleaded.

"I can't," he whispered.

Adam shook his head and William could see the exasperation in his face.

"We'll figure this out—you, me, Robert and Jason. We'll have the council backing us."

William shook his head. "This is my battle."

Adam sighed.

William stood waiting. He needed to make sure Adam was okay to get home—he couldn't have his life on his conscience. The last thing he needed was to take his anger out on his little brother.

"Why, Will?"

Will, a small word he hadn't heard in such a long time. The last person who had called him Will had been Emma, on the day of her death.

Emma, the other witch he'd failed—the other bonded mate he'd lost to the alpha wolf.

Shaking his head, William looked at his brother. Adam had aged in the weeks since their father's murder. Strange, considering that vampires aged at a slower rate than humans. William could see the outline of too much crap and not enough time to deal written all over Adam. His stance—his very energy—had changed.

He shook his head. This was not how their lives were supposed to be.

"I promised her I'd keep her safe," he said.

"The witch?" Adam said.

She's more than a witch. Katie is my salvation.

"I promised her, gave my word, and this is something I've got to do. Alone," he added for good measure.

Shaking his head, Adam looked at him. William stared back. He'd nothing to hide. This was what he had to do.

"What makes you think she's still alive?" Adam tried to reason with him.

Because I can still feel her. I would know if she'd died – no magic in the world would be able to mask that.

"I know," William replied.

Adam hesitated, glancing up and down the street. "Call Robert, okay?" he said.

William nodded. He'd phone Robert at some point but he wasn't ready to talk to his older brother just yet.

Robert had everything he wanted, while William was still hunting for what was his.

Adam sighed and William watched him disappear around the corner. The younger man shouldn't be worrying about this. He was no part of this war. William didn't want to be part of this war, either. He wanted to be with his mate and at peace.

Life didn't always go to plan.

William waited for a few moments, until he could no longer sense his brother nearby. He took time to gaze at the moon and the stars.

The stars, lonely and bright in the sky, with so much space to immerse themselves in.

"William."

The words whispered through his mind. He tensed, spinning around, trying to see who had spoken his name. No sign of life down the alley. William frowned but went back to looking at the night sky.

"William, help me."

He held his head as a sharp pain zapped through his skull. He screamed, lost and alone in the empty street.

Her voice – Katie's voice was speaking to him.

He collapsed to his knees, crying out in agony, not only from the pain in his head but from the pain piercing his heart as well.

"Where are you?" he asked the empty space.

For the first time since her disappearance, he sensed her emptiness, her lack of life, her resignation. She didn't believe he would come and get her.

"I'm coming, Katie. I'll never give up." He muttered the words to no one but himself.

William prayed that she would hear him, that she would feel his determination to get her back. Feel the love filling his heart.

But there was no answer. The buzzing in his head disappeared as if it had never been there, the pain leaving his body. William mourned the loss. He would have borne any pain to know that she was there, in some distant part of his mind.

Was Katie trying to connect with him somehow? He didn't know.

Was he imagining her trying to reach out? Had his insanity taken hold and ruined his already scrambled mind?

He would never give up, no matter what.

William got up from the ground and walked down the alley until he was out in the open street. Dawn was fast approaching and he had a few more spots to hit before the night was over.

Only then would he allow himself time alone.

Time spent dreaming about her.

Poppy watched the men from a secluded corner of the street. They were certainly not human, but then as soon as she'd seen them at the bar she'd known who they were. The Valentines were hard to miss. Their reputation preceded them—gorgeous and all deadly. At least, these two were sexy and dangerous.

She tensed, tempted to move from her secluded spot when she saw the crazy one—William—turn on his brother, the one with the sandy hair and shockingly expressive face. An aged vampire who still wore his emotions on his face was someone she would love to meet.

She tensed, wondering what she was supposed to do. She didn't want to see him hurt. He looked like he could handle himself but he was fighting his brother, being pressed against the brick building by the crazy vampire.

Moments later, after a brief talk that she didn't quite catch but that looked important enough to have the crazy vampire retreating into himself, she watched the other man leave. Moving down the street, pausing for a second to glance her way. Poppy felt her heart stop as his piercing green eyes sought out the darkened corner, scanning the area for a foe. Unable to sense anything — she wasn't his enemy — he moved on, not even giving her the time of day.

No man gave her the time of day.

Her eyes went back to William. He was broken, she could see that, but he was hurting and she understood the pain. Why couldn't anyone else see his raw need to find his mate? She could, and she wished she could help him, but she wasn't here to help one Valentine. She was here to help in the fight against the wolves and the coming war.

Once William was preoccupied with looking at the moon, Poppy made her escape and followed the other man. The intriguing one. She had no clue why she was risking her life but she had learnt something, even if it had been through eavesdropping.

As he turned to look behind him she ducked behind a nearby bin.

Once he continued walking, she followed him again. He was moving faster now. She tried to keep up. She closed her eyes for a moment as her hair fell across her face. When she opened them again, he was gone. Poppy panicked—her information was important. She'd got some bloody, fresh scars from the witch who'd told her where to go. The Valentines needed her.

The air rushed out of her as she was pulled against a firm body. One hand seized her neck in a death grip while the other roamed her body at the same time as pushing her against the wall.

"Why are you following me?" her captor demanded as he moved his hand down her body. Poppy shrieked as he cupped one of her breasts.

She struggled against him even as her nipple came to attention. Now was not a great time for her hungry body to come alight. The man was ready to choke her, for crying out loud.

"What does a woman like you want from me?" he asked.

She tensed. A woman like her? He hadn't even looked at her face yet. How dare he make assumptions? She tried to turn in his arms but he kept her still, his hand still threatening to choke the life out of her.

What an introduction.

"If you stop mauling me for a second I can tell you," she panted. Her nipples were puckered. Her breast felt heavy where it lay in the palm of his hand.

"What if I don't want to let you go?" he asked.

Poppy tensed again. She knew that the moment he saw her face he would no longer feel that way. No man felt anything for her once they saw the way she looked. He was pressed against her back and she was shocked to feel the pulse of his erection. It was the first time a man had ever had a hard-on for her. The first and probably the last cock she would ever feel. She enjoyed the experience for a second — she'd never known known a man who desired her — before reality set in.

He span her around and pushed back the hood of her cape, which had been hiding her from view.

This was the moment.

He looked at her face and gasped.

The stab to her heart almost winded her. She should be used to that sort of look. She'd lived with it all her life and this man was no different from all the others. But for some reason seeing him look at her with revulsion hurt more than she wanted it to.

If she had time, she would cry herself to sleep later.

"Who are you?" he asked.

Placing a smile on her scarred face, Poppy extended her hand. "Poppy. Nice to meet you."

He stared at her hand. She had scars lining the skin, just as ugly as the one on her face. Dropping her hand, she kept her smile firmly in place as she died a little more inside.

He hesitated. "*What* are you?"

Ah, the perfect question.

"I'm a necromancer."

Chapter Two

The banging was the worst part, as the prisoners were moved from one cell to another. She lay on the bed waiting. The clanking of the cages and the growls of the inhabitants filled the air. She was nothing more than an animal waiting for the slaughter.

Katie twirled her hair between his fingers. She looked at the edges of white mixing with her mousy brown. There was nothing else to do but sit and wait and watch her own magic destroying her. Twenty-three-years old and already she had white hair. Sophie had promised she would go grey first. It seemed strange to be thinking about something as trivial as her hair when she was trapped in a menagerie of immortal creatures.

Katie was past being scared. For weeks she'd been terrified, but it didn't matter either way—no one was coming for her. She had resigned herself to the fact that she was going to die.

The man who had brought her here was clearly disappointed. Day after day he came and forced her into a room with a just-turned male werewolf in human form. He would command the man to turn to wolf and...nothing would happen. Nothing mystical, no connection. She would stand and wonder which one would be the one to bite into her neck and end her suffering. She couldn't even attract a wolf properly.

What was his name again? The one who had taken her? The strange one?

Her mind was screwy these days. She couldn't remember a lot of things.

She remembered Sophie—at least, she thought she remembered Sophie. She recalled the name but no longer the face. When she said her name, she felt warm and happy. She was sure Sophie was a friend. She hoped she was.

The only person still rooted in her mind, the person who wouldn't go away, was William.

That vampire who refused to disappear from her thoughts. The vampire who had drained her blood and fed her his. The vampire whom she couldn't stop thinking about, the one whom she yearned to be with more than anything.

Screams erupted through the room. She turned over on the small bed, placing the only pillow over her ears. The man whom she couldn't remember, the one who'd taken her...he killed in front of her. The men who refused to touch her, refused to go near her—the man who'd taken her would simply kill them. She felt as though their deaths were all her fault.

A couple of the men had come to her and kissed her but nothing had happened. What did the man want? A medal for how undesirable she was becoming?

What is he waiting for? For all of my hair to turn white?

"Witch?"

Is that my name now?

She wasn't sure. Was her name Katie? The fuzziness was back.

Seconds later she heard her cage open. Someone grasped her upper arm, jerking her from the bed.

Katie screamed in pain and shot a ball of fire from her palm. She cried as the man holding her bit down on her arm, his canine teeth stopping any further attack from her. Katie welcomed the agony. It let her know she was still alive and not lost in limbo.

"William," she gasped.

She was pushed to the floor.

"William, help me," she yelled. She fought the hands holding her down.

"Fuck. The bitch burnt me," one of her captors complained.

"Just give me the shot," growled the one who had bitten her.

A pinch to her buttock, then sweet heaven, whatever they'd given her allowed her to zone out for a little while.

Clouds drifted over her, slow and beautiful. During these moments, everything became clear as she was whisked away into a sea of open arms, loved and protected.

Whenever they did this, her mind always sought refuge in thoughts of William.

"James will not be pleased," said the one with the syringe, throwing it into the cage.

"She's still fighting—at least she isn't dead," the other replied.

They picked up her body and moved her out of the prison cell. Their other captives glared at them with disgust.

They watched her for days, taking her away, then bringing her back feeling exhausted and close to death.

She heard her captors talking amongst themselves.

"The witch could bring normality back to all of our lives."

"The sedative had to be increased."

"It's not our place to question what we're told."

"I can't help but feel we're doing something wrong, trying to use her as some sort of mating queen."

The guy holding her stopped and glared at his companion.

"You either drop that thought or risk the death penalty. Questioning our leader will get you killed. James is doing what is good for the pack. Either jump on board or fucking answer to him, Blake."

"I didn't sign on for this shit." Blake shook his head as he followed them into the room and Katie was placed on the bed.

James was waiting for them, watching as they settled her down.

"Please tell me, why she is unconscious?"

"She burnt me."

"It's already mending." James sounded scornful.

"It still hurts like hell."

"So the little minx still has some power? Leave us."

Katie knew, in a vague, half-conscious way, that the magic was taking its toll. Not much longer and she would be dead.

Sighing, James leant back with his hands behind his head.

"So tell me, oh great and wise one, where is my miracle?" He glanced at the darkened corner and

Emma stepped towards him, never taking her eyes away.

"If she's no good, why don't you just kill her?" She moved over to the bed. He saw the knife and, with the speed of the wolf he was, he got her neck in his grasp. He had his answer. Katie White was not the girl who was about to change his destiny.

"I've no intention of killing the girl. I suggest you put the knife away. You promised me something and if you don't deliver very soon, this neck will be snapped," he growled, applying pressure before he released her.

He sat by the girl, stroking her hair away from her head.

"None of the wolves reacted to her?" Emma croaked, still sticking with her lies.

"Not one. She's not what you said she was," he accused.

Emma shrugged, her eyes flashing fire. "The funny things about spells and prophecies, is the wording — very tricky, wording," she complained, her hands on her hips.

"Excuses — so many excuses. I want the one who will bond together the wolves and the vampires. I want them brought to their knees," he yelled. He grabbed hold of her by her arms and shook her. "You promised me this was my time. I killed for you because of your promises."

"I always deliver," Emma said, trying to soothe his worries. Then, "Are we going to kill the girl?" Excitement and anticipation lit her eyes.

James glanced at the sleeping girl, wondering why Emma wanted her dead so badly.

"No. A witch will always come in handy. Anyway, it doesn't look like she's got long left."

Katie watched from beneath lowered lashes. Who was the woman and what the hell were they talking about?

The sedatives were lasting for shorter periods each time they injected her. She was shaking from the use of her magic. While she was weak, every time she used her abilities she had withdrawal effects.

After a while they carried her through the darkened corridor, through the locked security doors, until they got to her cage. Strange that they hadn't used her in the same way as before. She really must be close to losing everything.

They dumped her on the bed, escaping quickly before she threw a fire bolt, or whatever it was that came out of her hands.

She watched them leave, glancing at the other prisoners as they went.

"Hey, witch. You okay?" Katie turned to the cell opposite. The occupant looked human, like her.

Katie nodded but refused to say a word.

"That's good."

She put her back to the bars, staring at her small square of space—the tight, trapped space.

"Does anyone know what their plan is?"

This was when the other prisoners talked amongst themselves, discussing some sort of plan James and his crew had.

She couldn't care less. She wouldn't live to see it. It was becoming clearer every day that she was not needed.

"Rumour is, the Beyer West pack are trying to take over other areas. They annihilated all the witches, and now they're picking their way through everyone else.

Demons, other wolves—even humans." She heard this from the guy three cells down from her.

"They must have failed with the witches. I mean *she's* still breathing." It felt as though curious eyes were boring into her back.

"She's special, apparently." She heard the sneer in the voice.

Great—from caring one moment to sneering the next. A wonderful band of friends she had.

"I heard they took on the Valentines."

Katie whirled in her cage, going to the bars.

"What's the matter, witch?" one of the prisoners said.

"I was there when they came to the vampire council. That man, James—he killed their leader."

Silence descended on the room.

The hairs on Katie's arms stood on end.

"When was this?"

"The same night I was taken. I was taken before the council by William Valentine," she told the group.

A morose, morbid feeling filled the room.

"If they've got to the Valentines, it will only be a matter of time before the pack controls everything," the man across from her said to the group.

They all nodded in agreement.

Katie didn't believe it. She couldn't. From what she remembered, Robert and William wouldn't let that happen.

She moved away from the bars, going back to the bed. The sheets were wrinkled and dirty from her weeks of captivity. She thought of everything she'd heard while lying there. So much information had passed between the cell mates.

Who had the woman been, the one in the room with James? Why had she sounded so familiar?

Katie rubbed her chest. Her heart ached. Not long left for her…it didn't take a genius to work out what the statement meant.

Tears welled in her eyes. She was going to die.

She didn't want to die.

From the crushing of her spirit within this hell hole, she'd forgotten everything but the pleasure of being with William.

Her strong, bad vampire. The first man to kiss her, to make her pulse race and her body singe with heat. When she'd been with William, she'd felt, for the first time, the stirring of desire. William had awoken her mind and body and she wanted more. Katie had hoped to lose her virginity before she died. It could have been her gift to William. She would give anything to still be in his company, even with his bad attitude. If she was outside with him then she wouldn't be in here.

She sniffed as tears fell in great waves, the thought unbearable.

The irony was that a few weeks ago she would have given anything to be with her parents, to leave behind the chaos of life.

But since meeting William she had felt not different but special. She wanted to live, and the realisation brought with it a new wave of knowledge and despair.

Katie wasn't ready to die.

Chapter Three

William slammed the door as he entered his house, the sound echoing off the blank walls. The sun was up and the search was off. He went straight to the kitchen where he kept his fine whisky — the strongest kind. He wanted to lose what little sanity he had left.

He twisted the cap off a fresh bottle and gulped half of the contents in one go. The strong liquor helped to ease the pain, or at least to numb it for a short time. His face throbbed from Don smashing it in.

William walked towards the carpet where Katie had collapsed after he had taken her blood. He could still smell the innocent aroma of her. He touched that spot, hoping against hope to feel her.

Was she still alive? Or was he deluding himself by refusing to believe that she was already dead?

What did James have planned for her? The potential list was huge. The only witch at the beginning of a war, she would be a vital asset. One James would use without a care for helping her to keep her magic balanced.

Questions filled and consumed his every waking thought. She was a new witch, unstable. Surely she wasn't worth killing?

Running a hand over his face to try and clear his jumbled thoughts, he sat down at the side of the room. His eyes never left that space where, a few weeks ago, she'd come to life within his arms. He drank gulp after gulp of the potent whisky, until nothing was left in the bottle. He didn't get up for more. He allowed the liquid to do its work. He refused to blink, tears running down his cheeks as the bitter loneliness broke through him. He kept his eyes on that spot. Like a child, he wondered whether, if he prayed enough, she would respond and appear. The middle of his living room floor remained empty and his heart broke a fraction more at the wasted effort and energy.

After a while, his gaze began to drift. He fought sleep. He tried to force his eyes open, slapped his own face, but nothing could stop the weight as he drifted off into a blissful sleep.

William opened his eyes. He gasped at the marvellous beauty of the meadow. He'd not come to this place in such a long time. William usually made sure the liquor drowned him enough that he wouldn't have to wander through this world alone. His subconscious world – beautiful, peaceful, built for him to walk around with his bonded mate as they slept.

Since the death of his beloved, Emma, his place had been corrupted by her death. A darkness had seeped into his soul and turned everything he knew to hell. With Katie, everything was different. His paradise was different now. He couldn't recall the lake, or the deer running across the field. The air smelt fresh, no waves of pollution.

Magical.

Mystical.

William felt the pull of the lake and he strode over to the calm, serene expanse of blue – the clearest blue he'd ever seen.

He knelt down to touch it, a single finger marking the placid surface.

William jumped back as somebody erupted out of the water, gasping for breath.

William gazed at that face and cried inside with joy.

"Katie?" he whispered, not wanting to disturb the image. He could live with her here, like this. He didn't want her to disappear as she had so many times before in his mind. He wanted this to last as long as possible.

She stood twisting the water from her hair.

"William." He heard the laughter in her voice as she said his name.

Getting to his feet, he approached the water, holding out a hand for her to take.

"No taking my blood, now." She wagged a finger in his direction.

"Not without your permission," he promised.

Their hands touched and any doubts he'd had came crashing down, rushing away from his body like a bad cloud. This was the person he wanted. The woman he wanted to be with.

They were mated in the most basic of terms, just enough to satisfy the council and keep them from hurting her, but they hadn't had the time to complete the mating, for him to speak the bonding words as he took her innocence and made her his.

He wanted to find her and make the mating complete. To feel Katie's naked body within his arms. To take everything she had to offer and to give her all of himself as well.

No protection, just sheer, naked need consuming them both.

William shook his head, trying to clear the erotic images from his mind. There would be time for him to make love to her soon enough. Seeing her could only mean she was out there, somewhere.

He guided her from the water, his eyes never leaving hers.

"You look beautiful," he murmured.

"I bet you say that to all the girls, especially if they're wet," she teased, chuckling at his comment. William blushed at the innuendo.

"No, I never do," he protested. He'd never taken the time to be like this with another woman. Not even with Emma. By the time they'd become a couple the trouble had started with the witch and demon hunters.

She smiled and for the first time looked away, blushing and shy, as he concentrated all his attention on her. Absorbing her into his mind; greedily taking her in.

"Is this real?" she asked.

William didn't care — he just wanted to stay there and be with her. "Does it matter?"

She shrugged, looking around. "It's beautiful."

"This is my world," he confessed.

"Your world?"

"Yes, every vampire can do this. When we sleep there is a place we can take our mate. Part of the first natural, initial bond." He smiled as a deer ran past them.

Katie was laughing, the sound sweet music to his ears. He'd not heard her laugh much prior to her abduction.

"So we're mated?" she questioned.

He nodded. "Partially."

"When?" The attitude was returning thick and fast.

"The night I took your blood..." He paused to really look at her. "The night you were taken."

Her eyes dimmed and a wind blew her white dress around her body. She winced as the chill bit into her body.

"I remember," she whispered. It was like she couldn't remember anything past him. All of her memories had grown hazy since her capture. The one constant thing she remembered was William.

William was about to ask her more questions when she moved out of his hold.

"Why is that here?" She pointed over the meadow to the dark forest looming in the distance.

William couldn't recall it ever being there before.

"I don't know."

"That was the first place I used my powers." She seemed shocked by the memory. "I remember." She turned abruptly, knocking into him. "Why am I remembering now?"

"I don't understand."

"When I first got here, I didn't know who I was – what I was – but it's like everything is becoming clearer. I can see and I know what's happened to me." Her voice grew louder and more frantic with every passing second.

William needed to calm her down. If she freaked out too much, she would wake up and this moment would be lost. He wanted it to last as long as possible.

"What is it about the forest?" he asked, wondering what had got her so spooked. It was just a load of trees.

She took him by the hand and walked with him all the way to the forest's edge. Even though it looked far away, in his world, the distance was only very short when thinking of the destination. William tightened his hold, not wanting to let go. He watched Katie as she hesitated at the entrance to the forest before shaking her head and stepping into the darkness.

William followed her all the way through to the centre, not talking but remaining a constant presence for her to turn to if she needed him.

"This is Beyer Forest."

William glanced around before he settled his gaze on her. "What has this place got to do with anything?" he asked her. It was just a forest like any other. Trees, whole, shattered and broken dotted the ground, along with a lot of surface plants.

She ran her hands through her hair and he noticed the streaks of white in contrast to the rich, dark brown strands that reminded him of amber honey. He reached out and touched her.

Electricity shot up his arm, making his body tingle. His head snapped back as the connection with her locked into place. His mind processed scenes as they ran through Katie's mind.

She was here with Sophie. Scared, tired and feeling alone. He saw it all – the snapped piece of wood, the fear and the first awakening of her power.

He also saw the shadow of a wolf, which Katie and Sophie had overlooked.

William severed the connection, looking at the forest around him. There was something missing – something he should be understanding.

"You created this in my world." Never before had he heard of a mate, human or otherwise, being able to manipulate their vampire partner's own personal universe. She had imprinted her experiences onto the sanctuary of his world.

"What do you mean?" she whispered, standing close to him.

William inhaled her fragrance. She smelt like ripe peaches and honey. Sweet and juicy.

"You're so beautiful." He tucked a strand of loose hair behind her ear, enjoying the touch of the silky strand. William wanted to run his fingers through her hair, wanted to awaken her the way she'd awoken him. After years of feeling nothing but death and thoughts of bitter revenge, he now had a light, shining brightly. A light telling him to move on, to move forward and embrace this new future awaiting him. Katie was his and he would never forget it.

Katie blushed and chuckled.

"You don't like me," she teased as she moved against him. William reached out to her, circling her slender waist with his arms.

"No, I don't, you're a pain in the arse," he said, his body responding to her closeness. He leant down and pressed his lips against her head. "But I could never hate you." His breath fanned the hair on her head. William heard her sigh, then felt her slump against him, defeated.

"I'm so sorry," she cried against him.

He held her as the tears began to fall. His only regret was that he was holding a shadow of her and not the true, human form.

"Nothing to be sorry about." He soothed her – or at least tried to.

"If I hadn't sent Sophie to the council, then I wouldn't be here now and your father wouldn't have been killed."

William tightened his hold. He didn't want to hear those words. Words of guilt and regret. He wished with all his heart that when he woke up she would still be there, so he could show her how much he loved her.

Katie had got under his skin. He needed her; craved her. He loved her. It seemed impossible but he knew it was true. A short time was all it had taken for him to become hooked. Katie was like an addiction he didn't want to give up.

This little witch had given him something to fight for.

"If you hadn't done all those things, you could have already been dead." His heart hurt just from speaking the thought aloud.

Katie sobbed harder in his arms. He held her as his heart broke.

"Where are you, Katie? Where are they keeping you?" He asked the questions he would give his life to know the answers to.

He was desperate, now. Having her in his arms had given him a new desire to find her and a new hope that he would.

"I don't know," she screamed. "Find me, please, William. I can't last much longer."

Taking her face between his hands, he stared at her.

"Look at me, Katie. Don't give up. I swear I'm coming for you. I'm going to find you and when I do I'll kill the fucking bastard myself." William made her stare at him, so she could see how serious and determined he was.

"I'm dying, William," she croaked, looking down at the ground.

William tensed. With her white hair and the weight loss, he'd known she was close to losing the battle.

Tilting her head up, without saying another word, he kissed her.

Her lips were plump beneath his harder ones. She gasped, opening up, giving him access to her vulnerable mouth. He tasted her, absorbing her delicious scent and the delicate beauty that was his Katie.

His witch – his woman – and no one was going to take her from him.

She brought her arms up and held him. He loved having her arms around him and holding her. He wanted this in the real world. But he was thankful for the moments he had with her. Even though it was in a dream, at least she was in his arms.

Their tongues danced together, tasting and touching. He moved past her lips, down her cheek, until he was laying kisses along her collarbone, inhaling her.

It was torture knowing she was here yet not here – but it gave him hope. At least she was still alive.

"Promise me you'll fight, no matter what, you'll hold on and you'll wait for me. I'm coming for you, Katie. I promise." His voice was fierce.

She nodded, licking her lips.

He groaned, a pulse of arousal making his dick harden, the response delighting him, as he'd given up hope of desiring anyone but Emma.

"Do you promise, if I stay alive and fight, that when you find me you'll take me to your house...and to your bed?" She gave him a saucy smile through her tears.

William growled, giving her another fierce kiss.

"Is that all you can think about, sex?" he asked, his voice teasing.

"I've never had it, and now it's like an obsession. I want to feel it with you. For you to be my first. Please, promise me," she begged.

"I promise that I'll take you to bed, and more."

"More?"

He nodded. "I'll make you my wife."

Katie sucked in a breath, looking at him with wonder and, he hoped to God, with love.

"Really?"

"I promise. A real wedding."

She threw her arms round him, laughing, giggling and finally happy with life.

William caught her head between his hands, the need to possess her plump lips driving him to distraction.

"What are you doing?" she whispered. He saw the shock but also the glimmer of excitement in her eyes.

"Giving you a taste of what's to come," he said.

Her eyes closed and William took her lips, plunging his tongue deeper into her mouth. He wished with all of his soul that he could be plunging his dick inside her pussy, to show her how much he desired and loved her. His hands moved down past her neck to the straps of her dress on her shoulders. Slowly, William eased the straps down, exposing her full breasts to his view.

He pulled away and gazed at the perfection of her mounds. William wanted to suck and taste her. To have her writhing underneath his hands in pleasure.

"I can't breathe," she said. William smiled. He knew how she felt. The pulse of pleasure was affecting him as well.

He knelt down on the ground before her and took the rest of the dress with him. Her chest heaved with each deeply indrawn breath she took. She looked like perfection. Firm, round tits he could suck on all night, rounded hips and a small waist. A thatch of hair covered her pussy. Everything about her was addictive. William felt like he was worshipping at her feet.

"Come," he said. "Sit with me."

Katie, naked, knelt within his arms. William laid her on the ground.

"You're still dressed," she said.

"This isn't about me. I'm going to give you so much pleasure you'll be begging for me to fuck you by the time I get to you," he promised.

"What if you don't find me?" she asked. He grabbed her chin and forced her to look at him.

"Nothing will keep me away from you. You're mine, Katie." His hands went to the apex of her thighs. Her gasp and widened eyes made William chuckle. The only way to distract her was to use her innocent body against her. He slid his finger between her molten folds with such ease that it delighted him. William wanted to drink from her, to taste her essence on his tongue.

"When I get you into my bed, I'm going to kiss every inch of your body." He stopped and pressed his lips against her neck. Her body shook beneath his touch and he pulled his fingers from her glistening cunt. William wanted to give her everything. "I'll drink from you and bring you to climax over and over again. When you're in my arms I'll want to see nothing but the beautiful, aroused flush of your skin."

He moved his hands and lips down her body, her nipples his next target. William circled each bud before nibbling on it with his teeth. So full — beautiful and perfect.

He kissed down past her belly. Her tummy quivered and he bit into her flesh. His hands went from her rib cage and down to the smooth flesh of her thighs. Opening her wide, he gazed down at her innocent pussy glinting at him. The scent of her arousal permeated the air.

"You're going to love me for the rest of your life," he promised. Seconds later, he swiped his tongue from her entrance all the way up to her delicious little clit. Her taste exploded on his tongue and he growled in satisfaction. Katie White was his for the taking. Her fingers gripped his head.

William pulled away. "When you're spread on my bed I'll lick you until your cum explodes on my tongue."

"What about you? I want to see you," she begged.

He needed to release himself. In one smooth move he got to his feet and dropped his trousers. His cock stood out, firm and hard. He moaned as she licked her lips.

William took his shaft in hand and stroked himself, the tip leaking his pre-cum. He gazed down at her weeping pussy and groaned. It would be so easy to put his chivalry to bed and take her, here and now. But he couldn't. He'd promised her and forcing himself to wait would be the greatest torture and provide him with the biggest need. No other woman would stand a chance.

He went back to her side and watched as she moved her fingers over his where he held his dick.

"Do you want to touch me?" he asked.

Katie nodded, not moving her eyes from his cock. William released his hold and allowed Katie to grasp him.

"I don't want you to lick me," she said. "I want you to play with me while I'm playing with you. Only, I want you to tell me what you want to do to me."

She was slowly killing him. Her innocence astounded him. Did she have any idea how erotic she sounded?

He cupped her sex and ran his fingers over her creamy clit. She'd asked this of him and he'd give her it. She ran her hands up and down his shaft.

"I'm going to get you on my bed. Tie you up so you've got nowhere to go. Your legs wide, showing your wet cunt. I'll

make you wait and beg for it and then I'll make you come so hard you're screaming with pleasure."

William circled her clit and ran down to her centre. He didn't enter her. The taking of her virginity would happen in his bed. With warmth and caring and knowing that when she woke up he'd still be there, waiting for her.

"I bet you'd love to suck my cock. Maybe I'll make you do it. In my house, where I made you mine. Would you like that?"

She grunted.

"I want your mouth on me. When you're dripping and ready I'll take your virginity and treasure it for all eternity."

He fingered her pussy and watched as she came apart, her release sending his cock jerking and spilling his seed onto her body. They cried out in completion and when the feelings subsided, he wanted to do it all over again.

Katie lay panting in his arms. "That was amazing."

"It was merely a taste of much more to come," he said.

"Please, come and find me, William. I need you."

"I'm here."

Then harsh reality thrust in.

A ringing in the distance.

"Shit, not now," William protested.

"What is it?" she asked, the laughter dimming in her eyes.

William was about to answer...when he disappeared.

He woke to the ringing of the telephone.

Chapter Four

"What the hell do you think you're doing?" Adam held the struggling female as he marched her into the Valentines' house. His youngest sister, Rose, stood waiting for him.

"Robert is waiting in the study for you," she informed him, moving away.

"How's Mum?" he asked, holding on to the squirming woman to stop her from escaping.

Rose sighed and shrugged her shoulders. "She's coping as best as she can. She misses Dad and the peace he brought."

"Where's Dawn?" Dawn was another sister, younger than him but older than Rose.

"Out. No one knows where she goes these days."

Adam nodded and dragged the necromancer down the hall to the study. He didn't bother to knock. He opened the door to see some of the council members and his brother Jason.

"Where's William?" Robert demanded as soon as he saw Adam.

"Doing his own shit. Sit," he ordered Poppy.

He saw her fists tighten as she pulled her cape closer around her body, covering herself up.

"This thing with Katie is going to get him killed." Robert placed his hands on his hips and stormed around the room.

"He's going to do what he needs to do." Adam would defend his brother's decision. Someone had to.

The other men in the room stayed silent, glancing around at nothing, whilst avoiding eye contact.

"What did you want, Robert?" Adam kept his eyes on Poppy.

"We've got some information..." Robert said. Then he stopped, looking from Adam to Poppy. "Who's the girl?"

Adam turned his gaze his brother. "She was following me and William. Says she's a necromancer."

"Impossible!" Jason spoke for the first time since Adam had entered the room.

"How dare you?" Poppy stood, her rage directed at the whole group.

Jason stepped across and went toe to toe with her.

"I dare because necromancers are horse shit. A bullshit theory." The aggression came off him in waves.

"Jason, back off." Adam pushed past him and stood between them.

"Get her out of here, Adam. She's a waste of space," Jason sneered.

Poppy pushed Adam out of the way and went for his brother. "You want me to prove I'm not some bullshit theory? Test me, boy, and you'll be sorry."

She barely reached Jason's shoulder. She pulled hood back and showed him her face, her eyes sparkling a vivid red as she approached him.

Adam tensed, wondering what the hell was going on with his youngest brother being aggressive to a woman. He shook his head. They really didn't need this right now.

Poppy showed the men her scars and the power within her eyes. A true necromancer could radiate a spiritual force that helped them to find their target when raising the dead. After a nasty assignment, though, her spirit self was taking a rest—she wouldn't be able to call it forth for a while.

Raising the dead was a dangerous business, especially raising immortals.

Poppy could sense this man's discomfort with her. He was afraid of necromancers, frightened to believe that they might be a reality.

Shaking her head, she turned back to Adam.

"I came to help you. I'm not going to take being insulted," she said softly, her eyes changing back to their natural colour, grey.

"We'll talk once I'm done." He helped her outside and found her a chair. He clearly thought she was in pain because of all of her scars. Poppy liked the help. For once, she could feel like a female with a man to take care of her.

Poppy watched him go back in and shut the heavy door behind him. She could sense the death surrounding the family. It hadn't been long since they'd lost a loved one. Necromancers couldn't contact spirits but they could sense them; feel them around. Whomever they had lost wasn't passing over. If she wanted to raise the body, he would be easy to find.

Her arm tingled from Adam's touch. She glanced at the door.

She wished she didn't have all the scars. But some dead bodies still had another fight left in them.

Poppy didn't understand why she was feeling emotional. She had no clue who this family was, but she couldn't stop the reactions within her body. When fate wanted to throw her into someone's path, there was nothing she could do to stop it.

She listened to the vampires in the other room, her body calming down as she realised she was supposed to be here. Being a necromancer heightened her hearing far above that of vampires and humans. She heard spirits from the other realm, for crying out loud. A thick wood door was nothing.

"What is your beef?" Adam asked as soon as they were in private. Jason glanced at the other men in the room as if looking for support.

"No, you don't just stand off with a woman and expect other people to fight your battles. Be a man and take responsibility."

Jason was the youngest male in the family and the most coddled. Even more coddled than the women. Even though Rose was the youngest of them all, she had been forced to deal with her own problems.

"She's a necromancer," he murmured.

Adam pointed at him, his rage surfacing. "I don't give a fuck what she is, you don't take to fucking threatening a woman," he yelled.

"Do you even remember what necromancers can do?" Jason stuttered back.

Adam threw his hands in the air as he glanced at each man individually.

"Last time I checked, brother, you were the youngest vampire in this room and had never even met a necromancer."

Jason bowed his head, embarrassed. Adam wasn't going to feel guilty. Jason deserved the harshness. He needed to be brought down to earth.

Robert finally spoke up. "He's right, Jason. You shouldn't have done that."

"Until we know what the hell is going on, she stays." Adam pointed to the door outside which Poppy was waiting.

Adam knew she was important in some way. What shocked him, though, was his lack of fear. He knew the rumours about necromancers controlling the dead and, with him being a vampire and all, he didn't want her controlling him.

Poppy was obviously a warrior, from the scars dotting her hands and face. He'd bet she had scars all over her body and, in this house, she would be treated with the respect a warrior deserved. She'd been through enough.

He hated how he'd responded to her earlier. He wasn't sickened by her scars — he admired her.

A woman of worth.

"I've got some information about the compound where they're holding Katie," Robert said to the group. "I want to know who's in and who's out."

"How reliable is this info?" Adam questioned.

"A source I can trust," he answered evasively. Since their father's death and the start of the war, Robert had been more like a commander than a brother. Adam didn't know how to relate to him anymore.

"You'll need to phone William."

"He doesn't need to know," Robert argued.

Running his hand through his hair, Adam tried to hold on to what precious sanity he had left.

"If you don't involve William in a mission to rescue Katie, you will lose him. He is close to losing it already. We need to find her." It was the best advice Adam could give.

"I'll come as well."

All heads in the room turned to the door.

Don was standing there in a leather jacket and blue jeans, his arms folded, everything about him the commanding soldier he'd once been.

"Well, I'll be damned. Don Hargreaves." Robert went over and embraced the older vampire.

"Sorry about your loss. Your father was a great man."

"You here to kick my butt?" Adam asked.

Don chuckled, shaking his head.

"I felt this coming—war with the wolves, right?"

"Killed my father, took our witch and pretty much declared war," Robert confirmed.

"Figured as much. You can feel the tension everywhere. I'm here to help," Don said.

"And me." Poppy was standing inside the door.

"What can you do?" Robert queried.

"I may be a woman, but anyone dead—young or old—I can find them and get the answers you need. You'll need me at this compound where you think the witch is being held."

Adam's heart raced. He rubbed his chest. He didn't like the thought of her going on a mission like this.

She stared at all of them. A bad-ass girl.

"I'll call William. We do this tonight at sundown," Robert said to the group.

Adam took Poppy by the arm and guided her out of the room, refusing to let go until he had them both safely locked away in his room.

* * * *

William glared at the light flashing on his mobile. Running a hand over his face, he mourned his return to the real world.

But he couldn't ignore his brother for long, even if he wanted to.

Flipping open the mobile phone, he pressed it to his ear.

"Yeah?" His voice croaked and his hands were shaking. He got up from the floor and moved to the bathroom. The mirror showed him how rough and unkempt he looked.

"Will, it's Robert."

"I figured that one out when it flashed on the screen. Call screening, Robert," William said to his brother with all the sarcasm he could muster.

"Whatever Will."

"Stop calling me that." Will was from another time — a nicer time.

"Fine, how have you been?"

"We're going to make small talk?" William knew he was being a bastard, but he couldn't help it.

"This is how it's going to be between us?" Robert asked him.

"While my big brother is trying to stop me looking for my witch, yeah, expect this." He splashed some water on his face, making sure he didn't splash the mobile, running the water through his hair, wiping the dried blood from his face.

"I'm phoning because I've got some info about Katie."

William stood up straight, waiting. "I'm listening."

"It's a possible location where she might be. Alive or buried —"

"She's alive," William interrupted him.

"How do you know?" Robert asked.

"She visited me in the other world," he replied honestly.

He heard Robert's hesitation.

"I know what you're thinking," William said.

"You saw Emma even after she died," Robert reminded him.

"This is different. Katie isn't dead. She's a fighter."

William knew Robert doubted him but he didn't care. Katie was alive and he was going to find her. "Count me in." He flipped the phone shut.

He stared at himself in the mirror. His sandy blond hair flowed in wet waves around his face. The stubble on his face had grown over the last few weeks. Shaving would have been a waste of time. He ran a hand over the growth on his face, not sure what to make of it. His eyes were lifeless. The sparkle that had returned for a short time while Katie had been with him had faded with each of his failed searches.

The one woman in over a century he'd promised to protect with his life and she was at the mercy of the Alpha wolf of the Beyer West pack. The fiercest pack in the world. The same man who'd searched the globe, murdering witches until no one knew if they even existed anymore. Katie had been the first one in decades.

Inexperienced, innocent and beautiful.

He wanted her for his own.

His heart ached to feel her close. He'd been with her for such a short time, her fiery attitude and crazy powers a warm welcome against this bitter loneliness.

He'd lost Emma and finally come back from the brittle edge of sanity. If he lost Katie, he would go over the line and never return.

This ended with Katie by his side as his wife and mate, or it ended with his death.

He refused to continue without her.

He jumped into the shower, preparing for the night ahead, the smell of peaches soothing his bitter beast.

Chapter Five

"They're coming again, witch," said the man in the other cage opposite.

Katie didn't care. She was touching her lips, where William had kissed her. Had it been a nightmare or a salvation, going to sleep? Feeling William wrapped in her arms for even a moment had been so beautiful.

He'd asked her to fight and that was what she would do.

"Witch." The voice echoed off the walls. The voice of the man who had taken her.

Katie refused to move, to give him any power over her.

She closed her eyes and pictured William. She wished he was here to comfort her.

"Witch." The sound louder now and closer.

When she sensed that he was by the bed, she rolled over and glared at him. "Fuck off," she growled, shooting her arm out to spit her magic at him.

He was faster and, already weak, she couldn't stop him. He grabbed her wrist and knocked it aside. The magic hit the wall and died. Wasted energy, magic and power. He jerked her to her feet.

"When are you going to learn your place?" he snapped in her face.

She kneed him in the balls. "When you learn yours, dog."

He fell to his knees and his grip on her arm loosened. Being with William had brought back her fighting spirit.

Katie lashed out and kicked him in the balls again, then ran for the door. He scrambled up and caught her around the waist, hauling her off her feet and tossing her over his shoulder. Katie pummelled his back.

"Let me go, mutt."

Her little fists did nothing against the strong back. She knew her knuckles would be bruised. His muscles were like rock.

He smacked her ass. Outraged, she bit him. He tensed and howled in pain.

Katie waited for retaliation but nothing came. He simply straightened up and kept walking.

Katie didn't know where he was taking her. She couldn't see anything.

He dumped her on a huge bed. Katie scrambled off to the other end and ran for the door, but he grabbed her by the waist and threw her down. Katie knew it was hopeless. Moving to a sitting position, she sent daggers his way with her gaze, folding her arms.

"A little fire left in you," he complimented her.

Katie turned away, not caring if it made her look childish. The man was a monster.

"Want some wine?" he asked.

She refused to take the bait, her heart pounding, her mind spinning. She refused to allow the panic to come through.

"No? What about some fruit?" He came to her side and tried to catch her eyes. Katie refused to give him any attention. But she decided against moving. He could still kill her at a moment's notice. She'd promised William she'd stay alive.

"Not going to talk to me at all?" He caressed her cheek.

Katie flinched away from the contact. "Don't fucking touch me."

He chuckled, grabbing her chin.

"The little witch has claws, does she? I suggest you be careful how you use them."

Katie pulled away from his grip.

"What do you want with me?" she asked him. She hated the wobble that erupted as she spoke.

"To get to know you."

Katie snorted. "You kidnap me from the Valentines, test me, then pass me around your dogs like some sort of prize, and now you expect me to talk to you?" she mused.

"What about it? You're beautiful. And, all right, you haven't done what I wanted, but there is nothing to stop you enjoying my company." He took a sip of wine.

Katie knew he was up to something. "I have no desire to get to know you. You might as well take me back."

"This because of William Valentine?"

Katie stopped and glanced at him, her body tight. She didn't say anything, just stopped and waited for him to continue.

"Ah, William Valentine. The second in line and the one who is closer to the devil than any of them," he said.

"You don't know him," she replied defensively.

"I don't know him? Little witch, I was there when I took his first mate from him. Emma. She was the woman he really loved. A beautiful, powerful witch who sacrificed herself in order to save him." He reached out to touch her again.

Katie slapped his hand away.

"You know you're powerful, too. Killing a werewolf with your own hands without chanting some sort of spell makes you powerful. You would make the perfect queen for my pack."

Katie burst out laughing at the absurd suggestion. "Me, be your queen? You think I've got some sort of Stockholm syndrome? I want nothing to do with you." She yelled the last part at him.

"Are you sure about that?" he asked, crawling onto the bed.

She backed away until she was against the headboard. He moved in closer. Katie tensed, not knowing what to do.

"I wouldn't touch you."

"No?"

"Never."

He was perched a breath away from her. "Maybe this will change your mind."

He kissed her. Katie fought him, but before she could stop it her mind opened up and connected with his.

A cave somewhere secluded in the Beyer West forest. She saw inside the bolted metal door. The dead human bodies.

She pulled away, scared, mortified and disgusted. "What the hell have you done?"

He tapped her on the nose, the touch somewhat affectionate. "That, my little witch, you will have to wait and see." He got up from the bed. "Oh, and I wonder if you'll change your mind then."

* * * *

When William returned to his family home, Rose was waiting for him. She ran to embrace her brother. William hugged and kissed her, showing his youngest sister the affection she craved.

"Where are they?" he asked. He felt the trembling in her body.

"In the living room, waiting for you."

He nodded and kissed her cheek again. "Take care, okay?"

Rose nodded, her eyes shining with unshed tears.

He smiled, trying to reassure her as best as he could. This wasn't his place.

A room full of twenty men waited for him. Robert was among them, Sophie hugging him tight.

"Better get this show on the road," William said. Rose went to kneel at her mother's side.

"What the hell are you doing here?" he asked Don, the man who'd beaten him the night before.

"Helping," the older vampire said.

"Enough, William." Robert kissed his wife and moved forward to embrace his brother. William hadn't seen Robert since their father's death. He could see that his brother had aged in the role of Beyer West leader.

William tightened his arms around his brother.

"You're both fools." Their mother's voice.

Both brothers turned to her. She stood, ignoring Rose.

"Mother. We've talked about this."

"Your father died facing this man—this wolf—and now all my sons are going to get this girl back. This witch," she growled.

"Mum, she's going to be my wife," William said, surprising the whole room.

"Wife? Do you remember what happened to the last witch you tried to mate with?" Her cruelty was not lost on anyone.

Don was the first to speak up. "Mary, that was uncalled for. You love your sons. Go and lie down."

Mary glanced at the old soldier. She looked close to tears. She started to say something else but stormed out of the room instead, Dawn trailing in her wake.

Rose stayed, glancing up at Don. "I'm sorry. She hasn't been herself." Turning to her brothers, she went each of the four in turn. "Please, come back to us." She kissed each man on the cheek, wishing them all strength.

William watched as she left the room.

"Let's get this party started."

Two hours later they were at the edge of Beyer West forest. The night was cold and bitter. William glanced around, constantly on the lookout.

No one spoke, all the men waiting, tense.

They investigated every sound before moving on. William noted that Adam stayed close to the female. Her eyes glowed red as they walked. The scars stood out in the light of the full moon showing their path.

William wondered at the connection between the two. Adam showed all the signs of a man protecting his woman. Tonight he would have Katie and everything would be okay.

"This is it," Robert whispered. A small opening covered by green moss, the metal double doors locked and bolted.

"Are you sure?" Jason asked.

Robert nodded, touching the door. "It makes sense. Abandoned in a place we wouldn't think to look."

William had his doubts. This wasn't a place of recent death. He hoped to God Robert was right, but his gut was telling him to run. To get away.

This could be his one chance at getting Katie back.

Don moved forwards and under his brute strength the lock gave way easily enough. The doors creaked as they were pushed open. Darkness greeted them, the smell of blood permeating the air. William began to sniff, to see if there was any trace of Katie. Nothing. He pushed past Robert, charging forwards, his impatience growing with every passing second. She might be in this room, even if he couldn't smell her.

The others followed, with Don and Robert close at his back, weapons poised and ready.

Where are you, Katie?

Adam brought up the rear behind Poppy. Some men kept watch outside as the others moved down the corridor, their vision tolerable even in the dark as they were creatures of the night. The silence was abnormal, the smell of death and decay strong.

William looked around and saw that Poppy was shaking. The smell was stronger with every passing step.

They entered a large room and William jumped as the large door slammed shut. He didn't have time to process the noise before he noticed bodies littering the floor. Dead, dried blood covered the walls, the floor and the bodies.

"This is not normal..." Poppy spoke loudly enough for everyone to hear. William could even hear the chattering of her teeth. "They're not dead."

Frowning, he looked at the bodies.

"What do you mean?" Robert demanded.

William looked amongst the sea of dead bodies. And he knew.

He backed away slowly.

"Robert, who gave you this information?" he said, desperate to keep his voice low and calm.

"A minion working for the council," he answered straight away.

"Whoever it was doesn't work for the council anymore."

"What?" Robert growled.

"Holy shit!" Adam yelled.

The bodies, the supposedly dead bodies, twisted and convulsed. William stared at them. They couldn't be werewolves. Natural werewolves shifted in a flash. These were twisting, the bones snapping, howls and screams escaping.

"It's a motherfucking trap!" William yelled.

Hundreds of bodies mutated into giant, ferocious wolves. Half-breeds. Humans turned by the bite of a natural born werewolf. Vicious, unpredictable beasts. Their heads turned towards the new smell in the room — the smell of vampire. The smell of the enemy.

William knew they were outnumbered. He tensed, aiming his gun. All of the Valentine men were in this room. Don, the next most powerful, many of the council members. This was not only a trap — this was an annihilation.

"Fire back!"

Gun shots and fighting ensued. William took down three wolves before he had to start using his fists.

His last thoughts were of Katie.

"I love you Katie," he whispered, hoping in his heart that she would somehow get his message.

Chapter Six

"Wait and see about what?" Katie climbed off the bed.

James spun around and looked at the clock beside the bed. He chuckled. He looked crazy.

"Well, you see, I sent William a little message about your whereabouts," he said, tucking a piece of hair behind her ear.

"The dead bodies I saw?" Katie panicked.

"My way of telling the Valentine men to go and fuck themselves."

"You're going to kill William?" she screamed.

"My dear girl, he's probably already dead."

Katie moved away from him, her heart racing, her head hurting.

Think, Katie think. William can't be dead. You promised him.

She paced, not caring what James thought. She had to find William. He wasn't dead. She would have felt it—she was sure she would have.

No, not dead.

"I love you, Katie." Katie heard the whisper echo across her temple. She recognised the voice. William was in a trap. She had to help him! If he could connect with her here, she could try to save him.

They were partway bonded.

"You evil, motherfucking bastard." Using her anger, her fire and everything she possessed, she drew on the elements closest to her. She shot her power at James. He was thrown directly across the room and through the door.

"You little witch." He charged her.

Throwing her right arm into the air, she slammed the door and pressed her hands forward to push all the heavy furniture in the room against it.

"Shit, now what do I do?" She stood and spun in one complete circle, bringing forth the power of fire. She was surrounded by a circle of flames.

She sat down, took a deep breath and thought about William, opening up the connection he'd made several months ago with their exchange of blood.

She felt him. It was like being plugged into another circuit.

Pushing past the last little bit of resistance, she found that she could see what he saw. The wolves, the blood. William was wounded, bitten by a werewolf. They were all struggling and had no room to escape.

"William, I'm here," she said to him.

He looked up, trying to find her. "Katie?"

"William, this is a trap."

"Don't you think I'm aware of that?" he replied.

"Unlock your mind." Katie opened her eyes, staring straight ahead. She released her mind to the elements. Wind, fire, water and earth. She connected with them. She could feel everything. She touched the ground beneath her feet. The window on the opposite wall smashed, allowing her a connection with wind. She had the earth, wind, fire and the pitcher of water. She was a part of the forces.

She felt the elements and she found William. He was so close it was unbearable.

"Open your eyes and trust me," she told him.

He dropped his weapon as the werewolf approached. The connection would only last for a short while. She knew her strength would give out.

The werewolf lunged to attack.

"Now," she yelled, and thrust all of her magic into his hands, their minds working as one.

William directed the magic, working quickly, spreading it around the room.

Wolves collapsed in a heap on the floor.

For five minutes she kept it going, her magic draining, her hands shaking. Her chest felt tight and her head hurt.

"Keep going Katie," he urged.

"I'm trying," she answered.

The last wolf lunged at the woman in the group. Katie tried to hold on. She couldn't. She drained and crumpled on the ground.

The door was flung open as she lost consciousness.

Their souls separated. She didn't even know if William had made it out alive.

* * * *

"Poppy!" Adam shouted, running towards her and the giant wolf biting into her side.

He put three bullets into the wolf, flinging it from her body.

"What the hell happened?" he asked William.

"Katie."

All the people who had made it limped over. Adam inspected Poppy's wound. She screamed as he moved the cloak out of the way.

Blood was pooling around her.

"We've got to get out of here," Adam said, scooping Poppy into his arms and securing her against his chest.

"You go, get home, we'll get the wounded," Robert ordered his brother.

Don limped over. "The witch is on our side, I presume?"

William nodded.

"That much power could kill her," Robert reminded him.

William turned and growled at his oldest brother. "You don't think I know that?"

William took in the bites on Don and the rest of the crew.

"Aren't those infected?" he asked.

Don shook his head. "These aren't full werewolves. Humans turned—their bite is harmless, but hurts like hell and slows the healing process. If a full werewolf had bitten me, I'd be dead within the day."

"That's good to know," Robert said. "Gather the wounded."

Jason limped over to the group. He was bleeding. "Where's Adam?" he groaned.

"Taking care of the girl," Robert said.

"The necromancer?"

He nodded.

Jason moaned. "She could kill us all."

Don frowned at him. "What the hell are you talking about, boy?"

"Everyone knows necromancers control the dead," Jason argued.

"Well I didn't think it was possible, but you've made me laugh tonight." Don tapped him on the shoulder, chuckling. "Remember, fairy tales that you read in books are simply that—fairy tales."

He left Jason looking at him with confusion.

"What the hell is he trying to say?" William looked at Robert with a raised eyebrow. He was the oldest for a reason.

William walked across to stand with Don.

"The witch is special to you?" Don asked.

"Yes."

They both looked at the bodies, which had changed back to human form when they'd died.

"Do you know where she is?"

William looked at Don. "Do you really think that if I knew where she was I would be standing here? I want her back. She's mine."

Don nodded.

"We're going home. You coming William? Don?" Robert called over.

"Yes," Don said, and William was about to refuse but the look Don gave him had him shutting his mouth.

Chapter Seven

Katie woke up on the edge of Beyer West Forest. The place where he'd left her last time. Her gown was the sheerest white and she was sure he would be able to see her body through the sheer fabric. She turned around, wondering where he could be.

She moved deeper into the forest, where James's kiss had taken her the night before. She examined the locked metal door.

William had to have survived.

"Thank you," he whispered into her ear, circling his arms around her waist. Katie relaxed against him, feeling him. William was alive.

"It worked." She breathed a sigh of relief.

"At what cost?" he complained.

"Don't spoil it, William," she pleaded with him.

"I won't. But what was the cost, Katie?" He sounded concerned.

Katie tried to think about the cost of sending all that magic to him. "I don't know." She really didn't. She hadn't even woken up yet.

He leant forward and kissed her cheek and she moaned, enjoying the contact with him.

"That feels nice."

He held her and they looked at the door together.

"I can't believe it was a trap."

"I can," she answered honestly.

They had come so close to losing each other.

"Come on. Staring at that thing is making me depressed and I don't want to be depressed—not here." Taking her by the hand, he led her through the forest, guiding her out into the open.

The sky was blue with white, fluffy clouds. Katie couldn't help but release a giggle.

"What?" William asked.

"Someone who is so serious has such a pretty place to hide."

He took her to the only tree in the meadow and pressed her against the bark, moving closer.

"I can't be serious all the time."

Katie felt his erection push against her belly. William took each of her hands in his and lifted them above her head.

"I have you now," he moaned.

Katie could feel the pool of heat spreading between her legs. He was so close and it felt...real. She didn't want it to end.

"I like you having me." She twined her fingers with his, showing him with that one act that she was where she wanted to be. Katie was no longer fighting to get away—instead she was fighting to get closer to him.

"I want you so bad," he growled. He pressed against her neck, feathering her skin with kisses. Katie shivered with excitement.

"I want you, too," she groaned as he thrust his pelvis against her. This was the first man who had shown an interest in her and she didn't want it to end.

She loved having him close.

Her nipples were hard, budding against the flimsy fabric of her dress.

"Touch me, William," she begged.

Taking both her wrists in one palm, he brought his other hand down, cupping her cheek, running his thumb along the line of her lower lip. Katie touched the tip of her tongue against him, tasting him.

She watched as his eyes flared at the contact and she retreated, not wanting to take him too far.

He applied pressure to her lips to encourage her to accept him and thrust the digit between her lips, observing her as she sucked him into her mouth.

"You are one wicked witch," he gasped, making Katie laugh. "I love that sound."

"What sound?"

"You, laughing."

"I love you making me laugh, William." She kissed his thumb, looking into his eyes.

"I love you saying my name—say it again," he instructed.

Katie smiled. "William... William..." She moved closer to his ear, straining against his hold. "I love you, William Valentine.

He moved his hands, sinking his fingers into the length of her hair. He grasped it in his fist and kissed her with a passion she had never experienced before.

He took over her mouth, her lips, showing her how wonderful it could be to love and be loved.

It didn't scare her to be in love with a vampire. She loved him so much.

She moved her hands to his shoulders and held on.

"I want you so much, William," she gasped against his demanding lips.

"I'll have you Katie. You're mine."

She gasped. She didn't want to wait. "Make love to me now?" she asked him.

William stopped, pulling back from her. He gazed at her and Katie could see him assessing her.

"What did you say?"

Katie touched his cheek affectionately. "I want you to make love to me, here and now." She moved her hands to the bottom of her dress, ready to pull it up over her head.

"Stop, Katie." He placed his hands over hers, holding the dress in place.

"Don't you want to?" she asked him, worry and hurt pulling at her.

"More than you can ever know."

"Then why are you stopping me?"

"Katie, my first time making love to you is not going to be in my dream and spirit world. When I make love to you, it will be with you in my arms, so when I wake up you are right there with me. I can make love to you here but it won't stick. You'll still wake up a virgin," he told her.

Katie cried out in frustration.

"I'm going to die a virgin. In this world wherever the hell I really am."

William took her to the floor, settling her between his legs. He leaned against the tree with her back pressed against his chest.

"Don't ever talk like that again." Taking her hands in his, he circled her waist with his arms. Katie loved the feel of him around her. He made her feel beautiful.

They sat in silence, watching the changing view, peaceful in each other's arms. Katie chuckled as he started to sing, his smooth, rich voice near her ear. She squirmed against him as a pool of heat gathered between her thighs, his notes pulsing through her, heightening her arousal. Her breasts grew heavy, her nipples sensitive to the fabric of her dress. Her tummy tightened against his hands. Moving her hands from under his, she placed them on the tops of his thighs, relishing the strength of him.

She held her breath as his thumb danced little circles across her belly. She waited, wondering what he would do.

He kept his hand on her stomach, not moving, and when it seemed he wasn't going anywhere she calmed against his touch.

"Relax, Katie, it's only me," he said gently in her ear.

"I can't. You drive me crazy," she gasped as he moved his palms delicately up her body to rest under her heaving bosom.

"The untutored witch and the insane vampire. We make a right pair."

Katie burst out laughing, all her nerves leaking away from her amidst the humour.

His hands lay on top of her breasts. Katie stopped and looked out at the scenery before her, seeing nothing but feeling everything. His comfort surrounded her; his hardness pressed against her back.

Katie groaned as he circled her nipples with his fingers. "That feels so good," she murmured. Her nipples budded, swelling as the flow of blood spread through her body.

The flush heated her skin, awakening her desire further.

"You're so lovely and full. You fill my hands perfectly," he complimented her.

"I want more, William."

He was showing her his lust and she wanted to absorb and taste every new sensation, as much as she could.

"You *won't* die on me and I'm going to give you something to look forward to." Every delicious word filled her with renewed excitement. "Do you trust me?" he asked before doing anything else.

"Yes, I trust you," she said without hesitation.

"Close your eyes."

Katie closed her eyes and listened.

* * * *

William gazed at her for a few seconds, just basking in her beauty and the love he had within him for his witch.

"William?" She sounded nervous and unsure.

He shushed her. Everything he had planned was meant for her pleasure.

He brushed her thighs and smiled against her hair as she opened a little wider to accept him.

"You have gorgeous legs, smooth and full." William saw her as the healthy woman she'd been after she'd fed on his blood.

"Is that your way of saying I'm fat?" she chuckled.

He tapped her. "Don't say such things. More flesh for me to nibble on."

She moaned. "We really are a strange pair."

"At least we've found each other."

He lifted her dress, pulling the fabric up her thighs, exposing her to his eyes. He lifted her with a hand around her waist—his vampire strength had to come in useful for something—and peeled the garment over her head and dropped it in the grass.

She lay naked and vulnerable to his probing gaze.

"Your eyes had better be closed," he warned.

He knew she had them open. His little virgin was new to all of this. He intended to tease her and bring her to him, to make her his.

"Should we be doing this?" she asked.

He placed his hands over her naked breasts. Her back arched and he smelt the pool of cream leaking out of her pussy.

"This is our world, Katie. I love you. I want to give you something to look forward to," he answered.

In truth, he'd fallen for her, the first night they'd officially met, when she'd blown up a werewolf. Her kidnapping, fear for her life, had finally made him acknowledge his feelings for her.

"I love you, too." She closed her eyes again. "I wish we were doing this in the real world."

"I do, too, sweet cheeks."

He showed her the pleasure he could offer her. Touching and teasing her; giving, but not taking anything. This pleasure was for her and no one else.

"It feels so good…" She cried out as he touched her again, touched everything but her pussy. He was saving that precious jewel for last.

When she was thrashing against him, seeking something she didn't have a clue existed, he gave in and swept his finger through her burning heat.

She screamed, her body opening for more of his touch.

"Oh…my…God," she cried out as he pressed her clit, enjoying the swollen nub. She was so close—with a few more strokes she was climaxing in his arms, holding on to William as the waves of ecstasy overcame her.

Just this once he was going to break his promise. No matter how many times he loved her body in this world, it wouldn't take any physical hold in the next. William needed to have her fully, at least once. He'd heard the sexual connection could awaken the senses and help to locate one's mate. Time was running out and Katie didn't have long. Even now, in his arms as she climaxed, her soul and energy were weakening.

He laid her down on the grass, hating himself for not waiting. Her eyes were closed and he used the time to release his cock. When he was around her it didn't take long for him to get hard. He pressed his cock against her centre, not pushing inside. Simply feeling the wetness over her pussy.

"What are you doing?" she said with a gasp.

"Loving you," he growled, before plunging his thick length inside her cunt. William pushed past the small barrier and knew she'd be whole again for him to take in the real world. Tiny sparks erupted between them and he knew this was binding them together. His soul awakened and her essence eased into him. William could sense her.

He kissed her and pulled all the way out before driving back inside her wet heat. The sensation was numbed in his dream world but would be like fire when he got her for real. This was a taste of what was to come—and his last hope for finding her. He rammed inside her body, the pleasure intense and unexpected. For years he'd gone without the proper love of a woman, forever dealing with whores. Katie was his and in his body he felt her thoughts and feelings. He smiled. Katie loved and hated him. They'd make one interesting couple.

"More, please. It feels so good," she panted. William gave her everything he had to offer, never letting up on the pressure, each thrust harder than the last. William gripped her hips and fucked her hard and fast. The need to come was strong and he couldn't hold back. He flung his head back and pressed his pelvis against her. His cock jerked and his cum shot deep inside her.

Afterwards, he held her, soothed her and loved her.

They were together. He'd pleasured her.

It wasn't enough.

The only way to calm his bruised soul, to save his life, was Katie. She completed him.

He needed to find her, and finally being connected to her, William knew where she was.

Chapter Eight

"Are you sure you're alright?" Adam asked Poppy as she lay, bandaged, pale but alive, on his bed.

"Perfectly fine," she croaked in reply.

He sat down on the bed beside her, the movement causing her to jerk, tensing as she winced. "Shit, I'm sorry." Poppy smiled. "I'm healing already, no problem at all. You'll be surprised to hear that what a dead person can do is far worse than the damage that werewolf did."

"So you handle this crap on a regular basis?" he asked, his curiosity getting the better of him.

"I don't know if you would call my stuff crap, but I'm a necromancer. It's what I do."

"So how does that work?"

"How does what work?"

"Being a necromancer? Do dead people just rise?"

"No, I have... Do you really want to know?"

"I wouldn't be asking if I wasn't curious."

Poppy stared at him for a few minutes. "Okay. There's me, the one you see, and then there's another me. I'm...like...split between this world and the spirit world. I call on the bodies of the people I need to speak with and my spirit self brings their spirit to merge with their body, and then the raising begins." Poppy winced as she moved to a sitting position. Adam was the first person to seem genuinely interested in what she did.

"So it's not as simple as it sounds."

Poppy laughed. "Do these scars look as simple as it sounds?"

"They attack you?"

"Some dead people don't like being disturbed."

Adam nodded. "I can understand that. I mean, I wouldn't want to be disturbed."

Poppy shook her head, smiling. The pain in her abdomen was fading as her body began to heal itself. The healing was taking longer than usual because her other half was still licking her wounds from the last raising they'd done. Well, not exactly a raising…

"The other problem is that I can't always control whom I raise," she admitted to him.

He frowned at her. This was the reason she'd followed him that night. The reason why she had been at that awful bar.

"The last person I raised was a witch…" She licked her lips, nervous as she recalled how bad it had been.

She had been walking home from the library. She liked the library. It was the one place she could go and think without interruption. It had been late and she'd walked past the cemetery. As always, she'd been able to sense the bodies there. Their unrest. A magnetic pull that she hadn't been able to stop had forced her all the way into the deepest part of the graveyard, occupied by the bodies of those who had died a hundred of years ago or more.

She had raised one nasty witch. Pulling up a body that had been dead for a few years was hard, but one that had been underground for several hundred years was worse.

A message passed from beyond the grave.

"She gave me a message to send to William Valentine," she said.

"What is it?" he asked, his voice growing louder.

At that moment, her spirit self merged with her, delivering the message that had caused them so much pain.

"Katie White is in danger. An old force threatens the coven of new witches. Katie is the key to the revival of witches, the vessel of the family magic."

Poppy could see his confusion.

"Wait, what the hell are you saying? Katie is the first witch we've seen in years. The rest were wiped out by James and his pack."

"James is not responsible for this destruction," continued the spirit within her. Werewolves can kill us but only through direct hits that drain our powers. Our family was killed by a witch," the spirit inside Poppy said.

"Wait, what? Who?

"Emma!"

Poppy felt her spirit self leave. Her job was done, her message complete. Shaking and cold, she pulled the blanket tightly around her shoulders.

Adam stared at her as if she had grown three heads.

"Don't look at me like that. This witch is the reason I'm failing to heal properly. I fought the message and the raising. She wouldn't let me. Said something about it being family, that Katie was family. A several-times-great granddaughter."

Adam left the bed and stormed round the room. Poppy wondered what had caused the swift change in him. She'd delivered her message and now the weight in her chest had eased and the healing process was speeding up a little.

"Do you know what this means?" he asked her.

"Well, no. I don't know you and I'm only delivering a message." Her tone was sarcastic. She had known the guy for less than a week and already he'd made her feel hot, made her feel regretful about her scars, got her chewed up by a werewolf and now had forced her into this bizarre war between vampires and werewolves. She couldn't leave now.

What pissed her off more, though, was that even taking all that into consideration, she didn't want to be anywhere else.

How was that for fucked up?

"Emma killed her own family. It must mean that. Holy shit—Emma has to be alive."

Poppy watched him freak out. He looked really cute, until he walked out and left her sitting here. All alone, Poppy wondered what the hell she'd done.

* * * *

Katie lay on her bed, shaking. She had used too much magic. Her energy was draining with every passing minute. She was dying. Her body still hummed from the wondrous dream. Being in William's arms had made her—for a short time—feel complete and loved.

Who would have thought she would find her soul mate in a crazy vampire? But he wasn't just anyone's crazy vampire—he was hers.

The end was coming. She could sense the other woman who was here. The woman who wanted her dead. Her power circled her like an endless serpent, wanting her blood, magic and life essence.

The other immortals in the prison were howling, crying out in pain. Something was happening. Something was changing.

"Katie," a still voice whispered through her mind.

Katie glanced around, looking for the source.

"I'm here, Baby. I'm always here."

Katie knew who it was. The only person in life—besides William and Sophie—ever to make her feel loved and cherished.

"Mum?"

Chapter Nine

William was close. He knew James. He'd spent most of his life searching for him, studying the evil pack leader, looking for a weakness. He couldn't believe he hadn't thought of this before.

James had a history of being predictable and lazy. He'd found Katie using her powers in the Beyer West Forest, the very forest where he'd killed Emma. He'd planted the turned humans, big and bloody. Now, as always with James, he would come full circle—and there, at the edge of the bridge, was what he was looking for.

No human eye could see the dark mansion with the iron gates surrounding masses of fields. Their father had believed this place was long forgotten. William hadn't thought about it, too busy dealing with his grief at losing Emma.

When James had disappeared along with most of the pack, William should have known that this was where he would have camped out. And he needed a witch in order to deliver protection for the wolves, a witch who could cloak the fortress in a sensing spell.

No immortal would even be able to tell there were werewolves in residence, though the spell had been designed to work against humans, at the time they'd been hunting them, trying to scour out all the evil lurking in the village.

He approached the gate and placed his hands on the bars. Closing his eyes, he allowed his soul to merge with Katie's.

William tensed, his fists straining around the bars.

She was here. Locked away. Dying.

William let out a mighty roar, his ferocious anger lighting the way. He was a beast, a vampire searching for his mate, and the Alpha in this house had her.

The gate bent and snapped open with a single pull. The first werewolf who came at him went down as he tore out its heart. A half-blooded werewolf was no match for the full-blooded, enraged vampire.

"Katie," he bellowed, making his presence known to everyone but not caring in the slightest. Six wolves came at him. He charged. The fight was on. He was leaving this house with his woman or he would die trying and he would kill as many fucking wolves as he could.

* * * *

"What are you trying to say?" Robert asked his brother.

"Emma is still alive. She's been working with James this whole time," Adam told him for the third time in a row.

"But we buried Emma," his mother said.

Adam turned to the rest of the room. Rose was standing next to their mother with Dawn at her feet. Robert stood in the corner with Sophie. Don, looking every bit the angry bitter vampire, stood with Jason near the door.

"No, we didn't. We buried a trinket next to her family. She's not there and she's not dead. She killed her sisters. She was working with James. She knew the location of all the witches. Emma would have been able to track them down." Adam began to get impatient.

"What does Katie have to do with this?" Robert asked him.

"Emma's sister was in trouble. She was pregnant. Don't you remember? She must have given birth before Emma killed her." Adam looked at all of them, begging them to understand.

"Fuck," Robert cursed.

"William knows," Jason said.

"What do you mean?" Adam asked.

"He left the house a while ago. When I asked, he simply said that he knew where she was. William is going to the fortress but he doesn't know Emma could still be alive. He's managed to track Katie somehow."

"Emma must have been at the council. She controlled us through magic so we couldn't stop him from killing our father. I'll destroy that bitch," Robert said. All the paperwork on the desk was flung across the room as his anger took hold.

"Something tells me that after Williams finds her, you'll be too late. When he finds out she endangered Katie — maybe even killed her — he won't come back from the rage. William is on a fine line as it is. A vampire without a mate and with all that anger will cause untold chaos. Emma is a dead witch." Adam said.

"I need weapons," Don said. "This ends tonight."

Robert kissed Sophie on the head. "Stay safe."

They all moved towards the door but Poppy was standing in front of it, the cape gone, her eyes glowing red.

"You take me with you," she croaked.

"No, you stay here." Adam pushed her aside.

Poppy grabbed his wrist and twisted, making him drop his knife.

"I was sent with this message. I have to see it through to the end," Poppy insisted.

"Bring the necromancer. She may come in useful as a shield." Don pushed past the rest of the group. His mission was to fight the wolves and to avenge his friend's death.

Adam looked at Poppy, seeing her scars, how weak she was. He should go and chain her to the bed, but just looking her in the eye he could see it would be no good.

He nodded, pushing her out of the door.

Tonight was going to be a mass of bloodshed and danger.

* * * *

"Something is happening," one of the prisoners said.

Katie moved from her bed, screaming as the 'something' shattered against the outside of her wall.

"Katie!" She heard her name being bellowed.

She waited to see if she would hear it again.

Please, please, don't be imagining it.

She closed her eyes as the tears began to fall.

"Katie!" Her name again, followed by the shaking of the walls and floor where she stood.

Her heart surged with joy.

"William," she whispered, chuckling when she realised how quietly she'd spoken. "William," she yelled at the top of her voice. Moving over to the bars that contained her, Katie wrenched at them, screaming his name.

Now that her freedom was close, Katie fought harder than ever before.

"William." She went crazy, pulling and heaving. But she was still human and the bars wouldn't budge. A witch didn't have the strength of an immortal being.

"Use your magic, sweetheart." Katie glanced up and saw the man across from her watching her efforts.

Stepping away from the bars, closing her eyes and praying it would work and she wouldn't blow herself up, she aimed her hands and fired. The metal exploded, disintegrating onto the floor. Never had her magic worked so accurately. If she'd known she could do this, she would have freed herself a while back.

"Cool, it didn't make any mess at all," she said, surprised, and left her cell. She aimed her hands at the other immortals in their cages and released them, too. Katie couldn't explain why she had more control over her powers now, but she was going to keep using it.

The man who had been trapped opposite her came forward and embraced her. Katie froze, wondering what he was going to do. He kissed her on the cheek.

"I'm forever in your debt," he whispered.

Katie pulled away, smiling. "Get me out of here alive and we'll call it even."

They ran out of the prison, charging towards the chaos.

I'm coming, William.

* * * *

William fought his way in the house, taking on as many wolves as he could. He'd been bitten by half-breeds. He was bleeding and bruised but moving forward.

"Katie," he yelled.

Pounding a werewolf into the wall, he yelled her name again. She had to be here. He wouldn't accept anything else.

"William!"

His heart lifted. Katie was here. "I'm coming."

He was so preoccupied by her response that he didn't see James waiting for him until he was on him. A punch to the face and another to the gut threw him back down the stairs.

"After your other witch, I see." James followed him down the stairs, a wicked-looking spike in hand. "Time to prove you can't keep *any* witch." He stood over him, the spike poised to pierce William's heart.

No, it couldn't end like this.

An arrow flew through the air and went into James's side. The Alpha wolf howled in pain.

"You, you little bastard, are mine." Don charged at his friend's murderer.

"I thought you were dead," James said, pulling out the arrow.

"Guess again. Go and get your witch, William. The others are here. We've got your back."

William nodded and ran for Katie.

The battle was in full force. He dodged werewolves, moving down a long, narrow brick tunnel leading out towards a row of cells, stopping when he saw a load of vampires, wolves and demons charging towards him.

He waited, calculating when would be the best time to attack. Then he smelt her. The wonderful smell of honey, calming his nerves.

He moved into view. The other immortals went in for the attack. He held out his hands in surrender, wanting only to see his woman.

"Katie," he called her name.

"William?" He heard the hesitation in her voice. The sea of people parted and there she stood — beautiful, alive and running at him. He opened his arms and she jumped into them. William laughed, smiled and thanked God she was still alive. He pressed his nose against her neck, inhaling her sweet fragrance. Convincing himself she was alive and in his arms for him to love and adore.

When she pulled her head back he saw that she was crying.

"What's the matter, baby?" he asked, his heart hurting to see her upset.

"I'm so happy you came for me."

The others moved away, realising how private the moment was, and sought out their own escape.

Katie made the first move. She kissed him, not in a dream but in reality. He lost his heart all over again. He moulded his lips to hers. Everything sang between them, lighting them up like the brightest star in the sky.

"I love you," he growled.

"I love you, too." She nibbled his lips, circling his waist with her legs as he pressed her up against the wall, mindful of nothing but her.

"Wow, isn't this all sweet and cosy?"

They froze in place. William opened his eyes. He knew that voice. He'd craved that very voice, mourned its loss. He pulled away from Katie and turned his head.

It couldn't possibly be who he thought it was.

William held Katie close to him but looked in the direction of his worst nightmare.

Like a scene out of a horror movie, Emma stood, her black and white hair in waves around her body as if it had a life of its own, her black eyes shining hatred and her magic pulsing around her, ready to strike.

William couldn't believe it. Emma stood in front of him. Alive. The mate he had long thought dead. For decades he'd believed he'd failed her. He'd killed her by not responding, by not being quick enough, clever enough or strong enough.

Yet here she stood, alive and enveloped by pure evil. It didn't take William long to understand what was going on.

Emma was responsible for all the evil that had graced their door.

The love he'd thought he'd felt died in an instant. With Katie in his arms he could see the true Emma, the one he'd refused to see all those years before.

What a waste of his life.

"Hello, darling. Long time, no see," Emma greeted him, moving down the hall.

William pushed Katie behind him, keeping her safe at the forefront of his mind.

"Trying to protect your little witch, I see," she said, still coming towards them.

"What are you doing, Emma?" He spoke her name, trying to convince himself that she was real.

"Finishing what I started. My younger sister gave birth to a child and I've spent centuries trying to find the little brat. Lo and behold my anger at finding that the child had been here in Beyer West, protected all along," she said each word, staring at Katie. The only living descendant of the child Emma was speaking of.

"You killed your sister?" He refused to believe it. The Emma he had known and loved wouldn't have harmed anyone.

"Of course I did. I was tired of being second at everything. The only way of surviving in this world is by being the best." Her eyes glowed as she watched Katie.

"Why?"

"For more power. Surely William, you must have figured that out by now."

* * * *

Abigail waited for her to come. Emma was too strong and too dangerous. She would not be able to defeat her. She prayed for the life of her baby girl, hoping against hope that one day she would be able to stand and fight.

The door rattled, then flung itself open. Emma appeared in all her dramatic splendour. Black, full-length dress, exposing the top of her heaving bosom. Her hair swirling around her. Her eyes the colour of the devil.

"Hello Emma," said Abigail, already resigned to the fact that she was going to die.

"Is that all you're going to say?" Emma taunted her, moving towards her.

"What more is there to say?" Abigail was calm and she knew Emma hadn't expected that. She stayed serene, knowing her fate.

"I don't know. Questions about why I'm doing this? You know – the usual."

"You're greedy. What more is there to it?"

Emma hissed, moving in front of her sister, trying to terrify her.

Abigail simply looked at her. She wasn't afraid. She had no feelings whatsoever.

"Power is not greed," Emma argued.

"That just goes to show how naïve you are. You really think you can kill all of us, store our power and not pay any consequences?" Abigail sneered.

"That's exactly what I'm doing."

"Then watch and learn, sister. You will pay for your actions and I'll be there to see you fall."

"No, you won't. You'll be dead."

* * * *

Katie didn't need to see any more. She knew what she had to do.

"You messed up. You killed Abigail, thinking that was the end of your line. That you would have all the family magic destined for generations to come. You hadn't anticipated me. Abigail had already given birth and, through the years, the female line was protected." Katie knew why, now.

"And now I have you, and to think it took my old mate's help for me to find you." Emma smiled maliciously at William.

"Why?" William asked. Katie could see that he was hurting.

"Oh, shut up. The Valentine with the lost soul. The lost cause. I didn't want you and I was tired of playing the good girl." Emma blasted him across the room with a simple twitch of her fingers.

Katie cried out and went to him. He lay gasping, clutching his chest.

"What the hell did you do?" Katie screamed. Then she was blasted away, out of the corridor to the top of the stairs.

The pain was excruciating, spreading through her entire body, stopping her from breathing. She coughed, choking on nothing.

"Painful, isn't it?" Emma spread her palm, then squeezed her hand into a fist.

Katie howled as the agony intensified.

Never before had she been in so much pain.

Her mind was being pulled, dragged away from the scene before her. She closed her eyes, begging and praying for help.

* * * *

"Katie," a voice whispered.

Katie opened her eyes, surprised by the lack of pain. She glanced around a room filled with hundreds of women.

"Am I dead?" she asked.

"Not yet, but you will be if you don't deflect her power." A woman stepped forward. Older than the others.

Katie felt the love she was emanating.

"I don't know how," Katie cried.

"Yes you do, my dear." The woman reached out and took her hand. Katie could feel her bloodline, the power and strength of it running through her veins. She sensed the elements and the love, the wonderful beauty of her magic.

"Now you know."

* * * *

"Scream for me," Emma shouted.

Katie opened her eyes with new knowledge. She glanced over at Emma and knew what to do.

She thought of a shield; an impenetrable shield of magic. A special protection.

"No," she said, her voice calm and clear.

The pain was deflected, crashing in a wave of useless magic around her.

Emma blinked, giving Katie enough time to get to her feet.

"They took you to the realm of witches?" she asked, clearly upset.

Katie shrugged, still unsteady on her feet. "Don't know where it was, just know it felt good."

"Don't attack, just deflect."

Katie made no noise to acknowledge the voice whispering in her ear.

"Cocky now you think they're on your side."

"Nope, but I can tell you they like me better than they like you."

Her anger getting the better of her, Emma sent a blast of magic Katie's way. With her palm out, Katie threw it off with ease.

"Sloppy," Katie couldn't help herself taunting.

"You think you're better than me, little girl?" Emma asked.

Katie chuckled. "Well, you are my great-great-great-great-great-great auntie. I guess at least I'm younger."

Katie had no clue where her confidence was coming from. She couldn't seem to stop the words tumbling out of her mouth.

"Well, let's get this started."

The battle began, Emma throwing magic at her, each wave more powerful than the last.

There was only one way tonight was going to end.

William needed to get to Katie. She was in danger and she had no clue how powerful Emma was. Decades of practice and the power of hundreds of witches. He couldn't believe he'd wasted years mourning such a spiteful bitch.

His head pounded from his being flung across the room. It had been years since a witch had done that to him. He staggered to his feet, using the wall for support, and started to make his way down the hall.

He could hear the screams and cries of the two women.

His heart stopped as he thought about Katie going into battle. The fear he felt for her had him moving faster. He coughed, bringing up blood.

A few more feet and he was out on the top landing, in time to see Katie flung down the stairs with Emma bearing down on top of her.

William watched, unable to stop it from happening. He could see Katie fighting back, pushing Emma away, using her magic to destroy evil.

"Time to die, bitch." Emma gathered all her resources. She was going in for the kill.

Katie pushed her arms out, forcing a shield out around her. This time the power was too much—she could feel the hot tingles as it worked through her defences. She wasn't strong enough to take her.

She screamed and cried out.

She couldn't do more than this.

As Katie was about to let down her guard and just let nature take its course, she suddenly felt the pulse of magic run back through her.

Hundreds of dead witches' magic was flowing through her, using her as a vessel, as a conduit of power against Emma.

One by one they appeared by her side, Emma's closest relatives, not the faceless victims of her greed but the family she had destroyed in the name of more power. Their spirits were waiting to deliver Emma to her fate. Katie could feel their pain, anger and thirst for revenge, but also the underlying knowledge that they were about to destroy one of their own for the safety and survival of the human race.

They became one. Their power combined, mixing together to become more powerful than any other force in the world. Witches alone were powerful beings, but combined together they were indestructible.

Katie felt the magic inside her. It was running through her and pushing out against her foe.

She looked at William and knew, in that moment, that she was not going to survive. There could only be one outcome of tonight—she and Emma were both going to die.

They surged forwards, throwing out the magic, as she accepted her fate, her sacrifice for the good of mankind.

She pushed away her pain and guilt and pressed against Emma's power, forcing her back.

"No..." Emma screamed as her power fell, giving Katie the opportunity she needed. She threw every last bit of their combined energy out through her hands, calling on the elements and all things natural to destroy this being who had disrupted the balance and caused untold bloodshed.

Within moments, Emma released her final scream as an explosion shook the very foundations of the mansion. Windows smashed as a gust of wind surged out of the house, letting in the wings of the devil to transport Emma to the fiery depths of hell.

When it was over and Emma's body lay lifeless and decaying at her feet, Katie felt the witches leave her side.

Katie looked at William one final time, allowing the love she felt for him to show.

He smiled at her.

She didn't want this to happen.

He moved towards her.

William made it just in time as Katie closed her eyes. Her body fell limp in his arms.

"Wow, sweet cheeks. I've got you." He moved the hair off her face. She must be exhausted. But he had his Katie in his arms.

He held her up and that was when he knew something was wrong.

"Katie?" He stroked her hair and he finally registered the emptiness.

He dropped to his knees with her body in his arms. He touched each of the points to check for a pulse.

William was holding the cold lifeless body of Katie White. The woman whom he had failed; the woman who owned his heart.

It was the greatest pain of all. Tears fell as he rubbed his face against her still neck, trying to inhale the last of her scent which was disappearing quickly as each moment passed.

"Can't be true," he howled in pain.

He heard the others approaching and swearing as they saw that the woman he loved had been taken from him.

He screamed and raged, willing Katie to come back to him, blind-sided by his own pain.

Katie had sacrificed herself to kill Emma, leaving an empty vampire in her wake.

Chapter Ten

Poppy watched as the men tried to soothe William, tried to intervene and take the dead body of his mate out of his arms.

His eyes, red, blood shot, turned to her. She could see his pain. Her heart broke as she wondered if she would ever love someone that deeply. The hurt of their loss would be unbearable.

"You can bring her back," he said.

Swallowing against the lump in her throat, she shook her head.

"Yes, you can," he argued.

Again Poppy shook her head. "I'm a necromancer, I raise the dead by contacting their spirits and bringing them back to their bodies. I don't bring the dead back to life." She held her hands up, trying to reason with him.

"But you could do it."

"No, I can't."

"I'm begging you."

"I can't do it. She would last a few days but then she would start to decay, William. My power is to raise the dead for a few minutes, a couple of hours at the most. What you are asking is for me to abuse my power."

The corpse would decay and the soul that was left would turn to nothing more than a zombie, craving human flesh. It would be ugly and dangerous. The longer a dead spirit stayed within the body, the harder it was to extract it and send it to the afterlife.

"But she's walking around there, alone and lost." Tears dripped from his eyes, falling onto Katie.

"Come on, Brother." Robert approached him.

Poppy wanted to help. She connected with her spirit self. If nothing else, maybe she could get Katie to give William a final message. Anything to help him in this time of torturous need.

Her spirit self searched for the missing link. If Katie was walking around, waiting to deliver a message, she would be able to find her.

But Katie was nowhere to be found.

Poppy opened her eyes and moved to William's side, placing a hand on his shoulder. "Katie has moved on. She is not waiting or alone. She has been embraced by the afterlife and taken into their love."

A crossed-over spirit was even harder to bring into a body.

"William, she deserves to be buried with respect. We'll take the body and lay her to rest like a mate." Adam pressed his hand on top of Poppy's to show his support.

"A mate? We didn't even get time to finish the ceremony."

William looked up, not seeing the people with the concerned faces, with the love and upset shining out of their eyes.

He looked past them, feeling only the dead weight in his arms.

Katie would have made a wonderful mate.

This was all James' fault. His thirst for greed, power and position had killed William's mate. He closed his eyes and saw visions of Katie in his world. In his arms, smiling, laughing and being the woman with attitude whom he'd come to love.

Katie had been taken away from him and he knew what he had to do.

Getting to his knees, he braced himself, taking Katie in his arms. He would put his woman to rest, then he would avenge her death and hopefully afterwards he would join her.

If she couldn't be with him here and now, then he would be with her wherever the hell she was.

Ignoring his family, he walked out of the door, resigned to his fate.

After tonight, he was going after James.

James was going to die.

Chapter Eleven

Everything was so wonderfully crisp and white. Fresh, light and wonderful. Katie opened her eyes and gazed at the fluffiest clouds imaginable. Sighing, in pure heaven, she stretched, feeling the burn as untried muscles protested slightly.

She giggled.

"William?" she called. But there was no reply.

Sitting up, Katie frowned. The room was decorated in the purest of whites. A single mirror lay frozen across from her. Katie noted her pale complexion. Her amber hair had flowers dotted through it.

Katie spun and saw an angel.

She was sitting on a window ledge with her legs crossed. Her blonde hair lay in waves down her back, all the way to the floor. Her eyes were clear blue and her voice musical.

"Am I in heaven?" Katie asked, glancing around wondering where everyone else was.

"Well, yes, you are." The angel turned, putting her feet on the floor and moving towards her. "Well...you are, but at the same time you're not. Wow. It still amazes me how languages don't make sense in this realm." Shaking her head, she moved closer until she was only a foot away.

"Where am I?"

"I'm Tara," the angel said, giving Katie her hand.

Katie looked at the hand being presented to her. Taking it, she gave it a quick shake.

"Huh, human protocol. Interesting."

"I'm Katie."

Tara laughed. "I know silly. I mean, I *am* an angel." She pointed at the halo and the wings.

"Okay, I'm confused. Where am I?"

"Well, you're in heaven but you're in the Seeing Room. Here, come and see." Tara took her arm and led her over to the mirror.

The mirror lay blank, showing nothing.

"I don't get it," Katie said.

"Really? In your time down there you seemed pretty intelligent to me," Tara accused, folding her arms. "Oh, for God's sake."

"You know, for an angel you take the big guy's name in vain a lot."

"The 'big guy' is older than life itself. The use of using his name in curses means as little to him as...Pluto suddenly being called a moon instead of a planet."

Katie held up her hands.

"What you are seeing is a window into the other life. Katie's last moments of life. *Your* last moments," Tara said.

The battle she had just had with Emma came flooding back to her, along with the pain in her chest. Katie placed a hand over her heart.

"Ah, it's starting to grow. Move your gown aside and check."

Katie really wasn't keeping up with the flow of conversation, but she moved her gown aside anyway. A tiny tree was tattooed on her chest.

"What is it?"

"The sacrificial tree of life. Sort of Adam and Eve's theme. Whoever wears that tattoo carries the symbol of a great warrior who has sacrificed herself in battle. She represents a chance for the world to start again and run smoothly."

The last moments of the battle started to play in the seeing window, freezing as the image of Katie turned to William.

"You defeating Emma restored balance between the good—being you—and the bad—being Emma. The death of two sides."

"Where is Emma?"

"Rotting in hell, burning for all the sins she committed. Even Lucifer doesn't like people messing up the balance."

"I don't understand what's going on."

"I'll tell you, but no interruptions."

Katie nodded.

"My job, as one of the All-Seeing Angels, is to watch over the immortal races. I've been paying attention to the Valentines, as they play an important part in the coming battles and wars of the twenty-first century. To put it simply, they will decide the outcome of this battle between good and evil. I know it's a cliché, but still, it seems that no matter what, every few hundred years or so, some party tries to ruin the balance set out by the gods and so a war happens, wiping out and destroying equal numbers on both sides. With me so far?"

Katie nodded.

"Excellent. William Valentine holds a key role in this fight, as do you."

"But I'm dead." Should she feel a little freaked by that?

"Exactly. You've messed with my plan. Well, not you specifically—that little glitch can be found with Emma who is now in hell and probably surrounded by lots of fire. I need you back on Earth."

"Why?"

"Wow. You really need it spelling out for you. William is useless without you—in fact he is set on a path that will likely kill him and the rest of the Valentine crew, knocking out the balance, screwing up the existence of every immortal on the planet."

"They're immortals, how bad could it be?"

"Okay, the reason there is a balance is because the planet can only sustain so much life force at one given time. It must balance to keep things working sustainably. You've heard of global warming, the economic crashes and breakdowns? It's all building to this battle."

"What have I got to do with William?"

Tara huffed. "Show William," she commanded the mirror.

Katie looked into the glass at the moment that her image fell into his arms. She saw the pain and sorrow. The begging and pleading as he asked for her to be returned to him.

Katie moved closer as the scene before her changed. Her body lay in a white coffin. He stood stroking her hair back from her head. She heard the faint whispers of his voice as he spoke to her empty body.

It's all because of him. After tonight, I'll join you, sweet cheeks. Wherever you are, I'll be with you.

Katie felt tears well and fall. He sounded so calm and serious as he leant down, kissed her cold lips and left.

"What does it mean?" she asked the angel.

"William is about to go and kill James. He believes it's all the wolves' fault."

"Why can't he kill him?"

"It is not James' time. You don't get it—things need to happen, revelations and justice must be served, but not like this. William Valentine will die tonight if you don't save him."

"I'm dead, how can I help?" Katie was panicking. Her chest hurt when she thought of William dying. She could cope with the thought of him moving on without her, living his life with happiness and love, but not with this.

She'd never wanted this.

"I need you to clip your wings and agree to go back into your body."

"I can't do that. My body is dying."

"You are William Valentine's destined soul mate. You can be reborn back into your own body, but it'll hurt like hell…and there'll be a catch," Tara informed her.

"What kind of catch?"

"You'll be linked to William and you'll contain all the magic you released from Emma. You'll have to control it. It'll be dangerous. The other catch is that as William's life mate and link, the connection between you will be stronger than ever."

"Meaning?"

"When he dies, you'll die."

"What about if I die?"

"The magic inside you will bring you back. It will all depend on William. That is the catch."

"Why do I get the sense that you're breaking every single rule in the book to do this?"

"Because I am."

"Why?"

"Humans, with all their whys. Because saving the planet and the human race is more important than protocol and rules. Sometimes, in order to make things work, stuff needs to get broken. Also, in a few months or probably a few weeks, I'm going to need your help, without question."

"Okay…" Katie didn't like the sound of that, but she was prepared to work with it to get William safe.

"Is this a deal?"

Katie looked at William, at the determination on his face. He wouldn't abandon her and she had no intention of doing it to him.

"Deal."

"We've got to work quickly. The preparation for your funeral took place last night. You've already been dead for twenty-four hours." Tara moved around the room with speed. Katie watched, wondering what the hell was about to happen to her.

"You ready?" Tara asked her as she pressed a sharp blade into her hands.

"For what?"

"I need you to cut your wings and then hold my hand."

Katie gazed at the shining blade.

"Will this hurt?"

Tara hesitated. "Yeah, it will."

Katie shook her head, turning her eyes to William. She began her task.

They stood at her coffin. Sophie was in the room. Katie saw the tears seeping from her eyes. Robert was standing by her side. She flinched away from his touch.

"Can they see us?" Katie asked Tara.

"No."

"Let's get this show on the road."

"Are you sure you want to do this with them watching?"

"Yeah. I always wanted to come back from the dead." Katie watched Sophie step away from her mate. She saw the agony on Robert's face, the guilt, and she knew in her heart that it wasn't right. "What do you need me to do?"

"Lie on your own body and match everything up—fingers, toes, everything."

Katie moved up onto the table, settling herself inside the cold weight.

"What next?"

"Embrace everything about to happen and close your eyes."

"Why am I closing my eyes?"

"It's easier if you don't tense up and if you think of William."

Katie closed her eyes and imagined William. The man she was returning to. The one she loved with her whole heart.

She screamed. Tara had pierced her heart with a ceremonial gold blade encrusted with diamonds, and was dipping her fingers into the blood and chanting. She couldn't hear the words. Katie was being pulled. She felt the thrust of magic consume her and agonising pain as her blood drained into the dead body below her.

Her body, soul and mind were reuniting, becoming as one.

"I'm so sorry Sophie," Robert apologised again.

Sophie shook her head. "You should have gone after her when you had the chance. The council…everything else could have waited and now the one person I asked you to keep safe is dead." Sophie was breaking up inside.

She looked at the corpse of her dead friend, knowing she had failed her.

"What is that?" Sophie asked, moving closer. A red blood stain was appearing over where her friend's heart was.

Robert stepped forward as well, inspecting the mark.

They both jumped back as Katie lunged forward and screamed, inhaling the deepest breath she'd ever taken.

She panted for several seconds, seeing the vision of Tara motioning her on. "William—where is he?" she asked the two people she had scared. At any other time she might have found it funny.

"You're alive?" Sophie rushed to embrace her.

Katie hugged her friend, clambering out of the coffin and jumping off the table.

"Where's William?" she asked again, holding onto the table, feeling a little unsteady on her feet.

"He's in his room."

"No, he's not. Where would James go?"

"William wouldn't dream of going after James."

"Yes, he would."

Robert looked at Katie and she knew he saw the determination in her eyes, her knowledge of William.

"James will still be at the old mansion picking up the pieces."

"Thank you."

Katie didn't waste any more time. She ran out of the basement and headed for the door. She heard someone yell, 'Dead witch walking' before she opened the door and sensed her mate's anguish.

Taking a deep breath, she knew he was already fighting James. She could feel and sense his pain; his anger and his raw need to be with her.

Closing her eyes, she opened the portal to her magic. Running or driving would be useless, but teleporting would be faster.

She recalled the spell sent down the generations, chanted the few words and disappeared along an invisible path to rescue her mate.

Chapter Twelve

"You knew if you stayed here I'd come back for you." William had entered the ruined mansion seconds ago. James stood amongst his pack looking calm and relaxed.

"Actually, I figured you'd still be paying respect to the dead witch," James said, stopping one of his wolves from lunging for William. "Or are you intending to join her?"

"I'm taking you with me," William announced.

"Just so you know, Emma fooled me as well. I thought Katie was meant for me and my pack but the prophecy didn't say anything about a witch. I was too impatient. I didn't want Katie—Emma did."

James was trying to soothe him. William was not in the mood to be soothed.

"If it wasn't for you, Katie would still be with me. When you realised what Emma had done you could have sent her back to me. You didn't. Now you'll pay the price." William removed his shirt.

James started laughing. "What are you—"

James was cut off as William went at him, taking him down in a heap. The wolves around them turned, circling their master, waiting for the opportunity to take the vampire out.

William didn't care. He wanted this wolf's head.

He kept Katie in his mind. Thinking about her kept her real to him. He was doing this for her.

William struck first, pummelling James's face with his fist. James reared back, instantly bloody.

William kept hitting the beast until James lunged, his teeth piercing the skin, the deadly strike of animal's canines going through the flesh to the bone.

The death strike, between wolf and vampire.

William howled in pain but nothing more. He knew he would die soon anyway and the attack had put James at a bad angle.

He sank his teeth into the wolf's neck, tasting his blood.

What the fuck?

James wasn't Alpha. James was a fucking half-breed.

Before William could understand what he'd found out, the wolves around them growled, ready to lunge.

"Quiet!" The yell echoed through the hall.

He knew that voice. Moving away from James, he got to his feet and turned to see Katie standing in the doorway.

"You're dead," he said.

"Well, I love you too, sweetheart."

James cursed, obviously knowing his secret had just been discovered. He staggered to his feet, retreat the only thing on his mind.

"This isn't over Valentine," he growled, moving away and towards the door.

William scarcely noticed James running away. He only had eyes for Katie.

"Have I died and gone to heaven?" he asked, walking over the smashed glass to her.

Katie snorted. "That is such a bad line."

"Forgive me, but wherever you are, it feels like heaven." He stopped before her and just stood there, looking at her.

Katie smiled at him, taking his hand in her own and pressing it against her cheek. "I'm here and alive."

He moved to surround her with his arms. She closed her eyes, enjoying the feel of him against her. He smelt so good. She never wanted to leave the comfort of his embrace.

"How can this be possible?" he whispered against her temple, kissing her hair. He ran his hands up and down her back.

"A second chance and a wish from an angel." She looked up at him, wondering how he would take it.

He frowned. "What does that mean?"

"I'll tell you later. You going to kiss me, sugar plum?" she teased.

He chuckled, moving to take possession of her lips. Katie moaned as he invaded her senses and loved her with his lips and tongue. She opened her mouth slightly, giving him sweet possession of her mouth.

"You taste so good." He pulled back for long enough to speak to her.

Katie smiled, weaving her hands into his hair to pull him down for more.

"I've been kidnapped, tortured, attacked and killed by your ex-mate and gone to heaven to be reborn and save you. Don't stop kissing me," she ordered before he took control with his lips, showing her how much he missed and loved her.

William moaned as he moved his hand from her face, down her neck, to cover one smooth, firm breast. Katie moaned, thrusting against his mouth. She wanted to feel him on her naked skin, loving her.

A cough interrupted their sweeping passion. Katie buried her head against his chest, her cheeks flushed and red.

"I take it Katie got to you in time," she heard Robert say.

She knew William was smiling even before she looked up.

"She certainly did."

"We've got much to discuss," Robert said to them both.

William and Katie shook their heads.

"Not tonight. I've got plans tonight," William said, never taking his eyes from her. Her heart stopped in her chest. Was he going to…?

"What are your plans?" One of the men at the doorway asked.

"I'm going to mate the woman I love with all of my heart and soul."

Katie smiled and went up on her tiptoes to kiss him. He was the first and only man she would ever love, in all of her life.

Everything else could wait. They would face it together as a team.

* * * *

Tara watched the happy couple. The battle had worked in their favour. They were in love and walking out of what was left of the wolf house, about to start their new life. She breathed a sigh of relief. At least she'd been able to help. She was so pleased she'd been able to keep up the attitude with Katie. When she'd watched the scene play out she'd had to look away, or she knew she would have broken down. She loved happy endings and knew that sending Katie back would do much more good than harm.

After all, William would have been dead and unable to relay his discovery that James was a mongrel to the others. Sighing, she wondered how things were going to turn out. Even an angel couldn't change anything until it had taken place.

"So, you interfered with the natural order of things. That witch was supposed to stay dead."

Tara glanced over at Limbo. He controlled the places between heaven and hell.

"You know I didn't have a choice. I had to help." Tara pulled herself up to her full height, which was nothing compared to his full six foot six.

"You had a choice but you refuse to allow this miserable planet to go."

It was common knowledge that Limbo wanted humans and immortals wiped from the earth.

"You will be punished for this," he said.

"Until then, get out of my room," she told him, turning her back on him.

Chapter Thirteen

Later that night after the formal mating ritual of William and Katie

Katie was mated. William was carrying her up to his room. They had already started the ritual on that night long ago at his house.

"I can walk," she whispered against his throat, her spread hand playing automatically with the hairs at his nape.

"I want to feel you in my arms."

Katie let out a giggle as he kicked his door open. They entered the room and he slammed the door closed with the heel of his boot. He moved to place her on the edge of the bed.

Katie swallowed past the lump in her throat. She wanted William more than she wanted to take her next breath.

"You're mine now, Mrs Katie Valentine." He kissed her lips, thrusting his tongue into her mouth.

Katie moaned as he took her mouth, tasting him on her lips.

She pulled back. "Really? Mrs Valentine? I didn't see a church," she teased.

He chuckled, sitting next to her on the bed. "Might not have been a church but in my heart you'll always be my wife."

The tears came to her eyes. Such sweet and tender words.

He cupped her cheeks between his large palms. "Please don't cry."

Katie loved him as he kissed each of her cheeks, then her eyes, kissing away her tears.

"I'm not sad. I'm just so happy."

"I could have lost you," he whispered as he buried his face in her neck, absorbing her scent.

She chuckled. "I'm here."

"But I could have lost you. I *did* lose you." Katie closed her eyes as she felt him kiss her neck. She had to tell him.

"There are a few conditions to me being here…" she began.

William pulled back, concern instantly written all over his face.

"It's nothing bad," she tried to reassure him.

"What is it? Then *I'll* decide if it's good or bad," he said.

Looking away for a second, Katie wondered what would be the best way to tell him. "I struck a deal. Well, not a deal. I was ordered, in a way, to come back." She glanced at his puzzled expression. "Just hear me out. This will sound completely crazy, I know, but just listen."

She told him about the angel, Tara, and everything she'd said, about the upcoming battle, finishing with the condition that when William passed away, she would as well.

"I can't let you do that—" he began to argue.

"I've already done it, made the deal. Besides, when you go, I won't want to stay behind."

William sat next to her on the bed and grasped her hand between his, kissing the knuckles. "I love you so damn much."

Katie smiled, enjoying his attention. Soon he moved from her knuckles to the tender, delicate pulse on the inside of her wrist. Slowly, caress by agonising caress, his touch moved up her arm until he kissed her on the neck, nipping the flesh. Her breath caught in her throat. Katie couldn't move. He made her stomach flutter, her pussy heat as her nipples tightened to unbearable peaks.

Goosebumps erupted along every inch of skin. She knew her pale skin would be showing the blush she felt spreading through her.

"You're so turned on right now," he growled, making her jump.

William placed his hand on her thigh, the contrast of the silky white fabric with her smooth, creamy thighs peeking out of the bottom against his large, very masculine hand made her legs shake. Katie didn't know where to rest her hands, so she leant back against the sheet, watching his hand as his fingers circled the edge of her gown. She waited, watching, wondering what he would do next.

"You're so beautiful," William whispered as he took her lips in a searing kiss. Katie realised he wasn't watching his hands—he was watching her.

She gazed into his eyes, wondering what he was feeling. Her body was a jumbling mass of nerves.

Without speaking, William took her hand and rested it against his shaft. He hissed as instinctively she curled her fingers around him.

"I want you so badly I could burst," he confessed to her. Katie saw the emotion in his eyes, the agonising need, and she wasn't afraid. She wanted to be near him, to love him.

He placed his hand back on her leg and moved his fingers up under the fabric covering her legs, up the smooth inner skin of her upper thigh, and rested them against her mound. The only thing separating him from her was the cotton of her panties.

"Take me, William. Make me yours," she whispered against his lips.

All she had dreamt about since meeting this strange, crazy vampire was being with him. She knew that now — knew the fear and the exhilaration had come from being near him. William Valentine was her everything and by some strange trick of fate she was his. With the coming battles and the coming war, she didn't have time to wait, to wonder, or have the delightful long courtship she'd always dreamt about. Life was uncertain in these trying times. If William and she made it through, it would be wonderful, but if they didn't then she would regret waiting; regret not acting on these glorious feelings consuming her.

She had no time, no room for second guessing. She gasped with pleasure as he pressed his fingers against her swollen clit through the damp panties.

Katie gave herself up to him, and she did it willingly, with all the love in her heart.

William saw through his heavy-lidded eyes the pleasure that his simple touch evoked in his innocent bride.

Katie had given him back hope, his life and, not least, she had given him the chance to love again. He would cherish her, look after her, love her for the rest of his life.

"This is for you," he told her as he moved away from her off the bed. He needed the distance to allow him to make it as good for her as possible. He would complete the binding by taking her virginity and saying the words. He wouldn't be able to complete it if she was hurting.

She sat up on the bed, watching him as he removed his shirt. William smiled as her eyes caught each muscle of his chest. He was sure she was counting. He went to her, pulling her up off the bed and into his arms. He secured her there against his body, in the warmth he felt for this woman.

Her eyes met his and he lost himself. He sealed her lips with his as he reached down, removing her gown, breaking the kiss to pull it up and over her head. She wore no bra and her full breasts were exposed for him to see. He cupped the weight in his hands, flicking the tips of her nipples with his thumbs. She hissed against his touch and she pressed more fully against him.

His little witch was becoming impatient to feel more of him.

"Patience, my dear," he chuckled as he moved her, bringing her body against his.

"I've waited for over twenty-three years, William. Please don't make me wait any more."

She sounded so desperate that he took her at her word. He pulled the panties off and lifted her in his arms as he placed her on the centre of the bed. Within seconds he had removed the rest of his own clothing, not drawing it out. There would be time for that later. Now he wanted to feel everything with her.

He moved onto his side, resting his head on his hand so his other was free to do with as he wanted.

He began by cupping her cheek. This was his seduction of Katie, after waiting weeks to be with her. He plunged his tongue between her quivering lips, melding them together as they had always been meant to be.

He kept her lips occupied as he cupped her right breast, feeling the nipple, moving to her left breast and giving it the same attention. Once she was gasping and arching against his touch, he moved further down, swirling his fingers along her tummy. It shook and tightened as he smoothed a path from one hip bone to the other until he dipped his finger down and circled her swollen, dripping wet clit.

She whimpered against him, covering his hand which was touching her pussy. With the speed of a vampire he grasped both her hands in one of his and pinned them against the bed above her head. She tried to break free of the trap he'd set. His strength came in handy. With his other hand, he pressed between her thighs.

"Do you trust me?" he asked.

She stopped her struggling for a split second as his meaning took effect. "I trust you with my very life."

"Then stop struggling and trust me to give you pleasure. To make your first time a time you will never forget."

She pouted. He smiled but refused to do anything more. He could smell her heady fragrance but he kept his finger still even as she tried to move her hips to get him to help her.

William rewarded her instantly as he moved his finger over her clit. She opened her legs wider to accommodate him. He still had her hands cuffed in his.

"Keep your hands there and don't move," he ordered her. He waited until he got her nod of understanding.

He kissed her one last time as he moved down her body, going straight for what he wanted. Using his large hands, he separated her legs, getting himself comfortable. He looked up at his woman.

He fell in love all over again. She was beautiful everywhere. Her plump lips were dusted with amber curls, open slightly for him to see her clit, red, swollen and pulsing. William licked his lips. He was so hungry for a taste. He could smell the musky scent of her arousal and he wanted more.

William used his lips to open her pussy. Only then did he move his tongue through the slit, gathering her juices on his tongue. He heard her cry echo off the walls as she absorbed the new sensation of having him lick her pussy, so different in the real world compared to the dream world.

"Oh...my...God..." she panted every word.

William feasted on her, showing her the magical power of his mouth.

He held her legs open as she tried to shut him out. He wouldn't allow it—he needed to bring her to climax with his mouth. He wanted to taste every drop of her sweet cream.

"It's too much, it's too much, it's too much," she chanted, over and over. He circled her clit, taking the sweet nub between his teeth, applying enough pressure to cause pleasure but with the bite of pain.

He touched her stomach, pressing down, and could feel the muscles tightening as her release began to build.

He took her to the point of release and brought her back down again. He repeated this process until she was begging and whimpering for him to continue. He wanted her mindless, so consumed by lust, desire and love as not to register the pain of her first time. The pain that must happen for the blood bond to be cemented. In the dream world there hadn't been any pain, only a numbed sort of pleasure. Whereas now every touch, kiss and lick was heightened.

When he knew she was past the point of no return, he built up the sensation, drawing it out for as long as he could.

"Not again—please, not again," she moaned, obviously expecting him to deny her.

William smiled against her quivering pussy.

He moved his tongue faster, bringing her closer and closer to the delicious peak. She pushed her pelvis against his face, fighting for more. He held on, circling his tongue; tasting, flicking the small nub that created an entire world of possibilities.

"William," she gasped as it became too much.

He hurtled her into a climax so powerful that he held her down to keep her safe, riding the wave with her. Holding her, reassuring her that everything was going to be okay. Katie was still writhing with pleasure. William moved up, looking into the face of the woman he loved. Katie was uninhibited and showed her pleasure so freely that it made his heart ache. She gave him so much.

"I'm sorry, my sweet witch," he whispered, kissing each of her eyelids. He reached down between their bodies, grasped his cock, stroking himself along her juices, coating himself with plenty of her natural lubricant. He seated himself at her entrance and pushed his cock in.

He looked up into her eyes and lost himself.

"Do it, William," she encouraged him. She held on to his upper arms. Her touch electrified him. He refused to look away as he thrust all of himself into her; one long thrust inside her moist, tight centre. He felt the small trickle of her virginal blood as her pussy accepted him into her body, pulsing greedily, sucking him into her tight heat. He felt the tip of his cock hit deep within her.

She sank her nails into his arms. He knew he was hurting her — he hated himself for it — and felt her try not to move but instinct took over and she tried to push him away. This was what he'd feared — the pain he could see on her face.

"I'm so sorry, baby. I love you so damn much." He kept still as he the spoke loving words to her, allowing her to grow accustomed to him inside her.

"You're so big," she moaned and his cock jumped.

"Sorry — you make me feel loved with compliments like that." He leant down and kissed her.

She groaned. "Can't you make it go smaller?"

William couldn't control himself. He started to laugh, the jolt plunging him a little deeper, hitting her pleasure centre.

She tensed but within seconds she writhed around him.

"Soon you'll be begging me to get a hard-on, my sweet witch," he assured her.

"Move again, William — please."

William could see the desperation on her face, not for him to get off and leave her alone, unsatisfied. No — now she was getting used to his body.

He wanted to hear her beg, just a little.

William moved to get off her. Katie pressed her little talons in, stopping him in his tracks.

"Don't leave me."

I have no intention of ever leaving you.

"Tell me what you want," he instructed.

"I don't know how."

"Tell me to fuck you." William wanted to hear her say the words, at least once.

Katie only hesitated for a split second. "Fuck me, William. Make me yours."

Pulling all the way out of her, William kept his eyes firmly on hers as he ploughed back inside.

They both cried out as they accepted each other. Katie held on as William took charge, fucking her for the first time.

Her body opened for him and tightened around his hard cock when he pulled most of the way out.

William took her on a rollercoaster ride, taking control of their love-making.

"Watch us—watch me take you," he told her, moving enough that she could watch as he fucked her, took her and made her his. Could watch his shaft as he pulled out, glistening with her cream. He knew he wouldn't be able to last. His balls had already tightened and his shaft was thickening as it pulsed inside her, leaking streams of pre-cum.

But this wasn't about him. It was about Katie.

He pulled one of the pillows from above their heads, lifting her pelvis up to rest on it, creating an angle that meant he could go deeper, hitting her G-spot. Katie moved her body in time with his.

William could feel the flutters of her pussy as she began to build towards a climax. He knew it was time to start the ritual. They'd completed the first initial bond, of his taking her blood and giving her his, but the bonding wouldn't be complete until he took her virginity and said the words that made her his. This was the private part of the ceremony, between him and Katie, and he intended to relish every second.

Placing one of his hands between their bodies, he fingered her clit, pulsing and ripe for another orgasm.

He pounded into her, waiting for the peak when he knew it would be the best time. Within seconds, her pussy was swallowing him whole.

Now was the time to make Katie White his — truly his.

William spoke the binding words. "I, William Valentine, take Katie White as my bond mate for all eternity and let nothing part us. By blood, by love and by all things pure, I cement her to me for life." He bit into her neck, sealing the bond with her blood.

This was the moment to see if their feelings for each other were true. The brightest of lights shone out of their bodies, highlighting the room around them. He burst with happiness as he took a ride into a surge of love, happiness and all purest pleasure one could ever know.

Katie White was his true, blood-bonded mate. His heart had spoken the truth.

He drank her blood and felt the power of her witch, the hint of the death that would always cling to her skin, and everything wonderfully Katie — the amber of honey and the hint of vanilla. He immersed himself in her happiness.

"I love you," he whispered, not speaking the words out loud but communicating to her with the gift of a bonded mate.

Katie didn't shrink away — she'd known he would speak to her in her mind. Her head confirmed what her heart already knew. It was meant to be.

They reached their peak together and brought each other down, knowing that their love-making was as magical as a sunset, fleeting yet forever with them, for all of their immortality.

"I love you too," she whispered.

Before the darkness fell, she felt him slump against her, protecting her body and holding her to his heart. The heart that, if it could still beat, would be beating for her.

Katie awoke lying near a stream. She looked up into the surreal beauty of a sunset like the one she'd imagined while making love with William.

"You'll miss it." It was a little boy who had spoken. Frowning, Katie took his offered hand and stood. She followed the little boy. She didn't recognise him at all.

She went with him past the blurs of the woods, the ice on the mountains, the little boy getting faster and faster.

"Where are we going?" she asked.

Katie tried to make sense of where she was, but nothing came to mind. It was the land of in-between. An ocean of nothingness but distant memories.

"A new king is about to be born."

The little boy was talking in riddles.

"Katie, baby. Wake up — wake up!" Katie looked behind her trying to find the owner of the voice she loved so much.

"No, they said you would see." The boy tugged on her hand, pulling her back towards the clearing. She glanced back one final time before she was plunged into darkness…and into hell.

William shook her. She wouldn't wake up. She wasn't breathing. He was freaking out. He heard the banging on the door outside and didn't care. He pulled the blanket around Katie, trying to keep her modest as the door splintered, torn off its hinges, and was thrown across the room.

Robert charged in first, followed by Sophie, the necromancer and Adam, then the rest of his family.

"She won't wake up," he cried, not caring that his family saw his tears; saw his weakness.

Robert walked over to the bed and tried to touch her. William hissed at him, prepared to strike.

"William, I was just feeling for a pulse." Robert held his arms up in a pose of surrender.

"She's not dead," the necromancer whispered from the corner. She no longer had her cape around her and William welcomed her scars. The battle signs of a true warrior.

"Where is she?" he demanded.

"The dead have a spirit around them, like a black cloud. She doesn't have one." She pointed at Katie, then shrugged.

"Don't fear, vampire." Everyone in the room turned to look at the mirror.

William got up from the bed, not caring about his nakedness.

He approached the mirror. "Who are you?" he asked.

"I'm a friend."

"Tara?" he asked.

"Katie isn't one for secrets, then?"

William shook his head. "Not with me."

"Wait and you shall see."

The mirror returned to normal as Katie gasped back to life. William ran to her side, holding her as she took lungfuls of air.

"It was so horrible—they tortured him." She cried out in pain as a red welt suddenly appeared on her back.

She screamed, releasing the energy of all she had just witnessed.

Everyone in the room gasped as they saw everything she had seen, every image of slaughter deadly and brutal within their minds. Most of them didn't know what was happening, who they were seeing or what it meant, but each person saw it in their head.

William held Katie as the welt disappeared and she became calm as if nothing had changed.

"What the fuck?" Adam growled.

Don came into the room to look at Katie. "You've got her power. Abigail—Emma's sister?"

"I don't know what you're talking about," Katie mumbled.

"Yes, she has." Tara appeared in the room as an unclear shadow.

"How is this possible?" Don asked. He'd seen some crazy shit in his time but this had taken the lead.

"Katie had to come back—it was destiny for her to take her role in this coming battle. As Emma killed all the witches of her bloodline, she absorbed their power. That power had to go somewhere when she died. Katie is the bearer, now, and as such she will need to get control; to gain stability," Tara said.

"She'll die with that much power," Robert said.

"Only when William dies will Katie die. Let's hope Katie has a child before then..." Tara started to leave but turned back. "Oh, and that little vision—that was a premonition of what's to come."

Tara disappeared, leaving behind a lot of questions.

Silence surrounded them as they looked at each other.

"This shit is real, isn't it? We're in a war where uncertainty reigns?" Jason asked.

"Yes," Don answered.

"What have we just witnessed?" William questioned.

Don ran his hand over his face. He looked as though he had aged, just within the last few minutes.

"Every war has a point where it began—like a tipping point. That was the tipping point. Me and your father. Fuck. The entire council missed it."

"Donald!" Mary said, disgusted with his language.

"Don't, Mary. We fucking missed it and because we did, Robert is in the ground." Don yelled. Mary stormed out of the room.

"Anyone who is not older than fucking sin please tell me what the hell is going on," Adam shouted at the group.

"James killed the true Alpha of the Beyer West Pack. That was the tipping point. James is not a true werewolf. He's a mongrel. Part werewolf, part human. By killing the true Alpha, he appointed himself the throne. Problem is, balance is everything. Without a true Alpha, the war begins." Don took a breath, running his hand through his hair.

"How could you and Dad have missed this?" Robert asked.

"Because we thought Simon had appointed him, stepped down and died in battle." Don yelled. He stormed out of the room, the others following.

Robert took Sophie by the hand and looked at William. "Study. Half an hour."

William nodded.

As they left, Katie looked at the door.

"So much for our privacy." William smiled, trying to bring some laughter to her eyes.

Katie looked at the door and chanted a small spell. Seconds later, the door was back in place as though nothing had happened.

"I knew you'd come in useful," William said.

Katie laughed, hugging him to her.

She didn't know where she would be if she didn't have his arms wrapped around her, protecting her.

Chapter Fourteen

Poppy and Adam stood together in the study as they all waited for William to appear.

Everyone was stressed and it could clearly be seen. Don was on the hard whisky, slugging it from the bottle. Robert was pacing like a madman. Jason just looked out of the window, all of his anger locked up.

"Where the hell is he?" Jason burst out, losing control of his anger.

Poppy smiled. He obviously wasn't holding it together very well.

Robert tried to calm his erratic brother. "He's earned his time with his mate."

"The one thing I've learnt as a necromancer is that the dead will stay where they are. Be patient," Poppy said, attempting to reassure him.

"Listen to me, you filthy little necromancer..." He charged towards her and Poppy was ready to strike.

She was shocked when Adam stepped in, defending her.

"I'm sick of your pathetic whining. Get over it and get used to her being here." Adam pulled him towards him by the scruff of his shirt before pushing him away, standing in front of her to protect her.

"What, are you going to mate with her?" Jason sneered.

"If I did, you'd show her some god damned respect," Adam retorted.

William walked into the room.

"Where's Katie?" Robert asked.

"She doesn't want to be part of this and she's tired."

William closed the door behind him, acknowledging Poppy as he did so. If it wasn't for him already being bonded, Poppy could imagine really falling for the guy. But Adam had been the first man to see past the scars. She glanced at Adam's back for a fleeting second, wondering if he could see past them enough to see the woman dying to be loved.

Shaking her head at the silliness of it, she concentrated on what the group had to say.

"We need to find out what happened. We need to find the true alpha of the Beyer West pack," William said.

"He's dead. How can he help?" Jason queried.

"Because it all started with his death. We find him. We find our answers about how James was able to do this." William relayed everything Katie had told him to. They needed to find the Alpha. They were on the right path.

"Well, that means me, then." Poppy stepped forward, closer to the light.

"Why you?" Jason contained his anger but not his revulsion.

"I find dead people. How else are you going to find a really old, dead alpha without me — a necromancer?"

All the men looked at her.

"We should send a party," Robert said.

"No, you shouldn't." Katie was standing at the door. William moved to her side, supporting her.

"Poppy can go. There is no danger on this mission other than what she seeks. The rest of us are needed here. To protect Beyer West."

Poppy saw how attentive William was towards Katie, and a small part of her yearned to have a man think like that about her.

"I'll go with her." Adam held up his hand. "I can keep up to date with you guys and be there as protection for Poppy if something does go wrong."

They all nodded agreement.

"We leave tomorrow at sundown," Adam said once the others had left.

"I could do this a lot faster without your help," she argued.

He came closer, crowding her. "I'll be there to protect you."

Poppy gasped. No one had ever wanted to protect her before. He brought his palm up and stroked her cheek. She opened her eyes wide and struggled to find breath…then he was gone.

She touched her cheek in wonder. Maybe answering the call was going to open up a whole new world of possibilities.

* * * *

"Shouldn't we stay behind?" Katie asked as William took her in his arms and escorted her up the winding staircase.

"Nope, they can handle everything else. I'm spending some time with my mate and trying to convince her about starting a wave of little vampire witches for the next generation," he teased.

Within seconds he had them both naked and in bed, luxuriating in the heady feelings of each other.

"I don't want you going through that again," he said as they held each other.

"I signed on for this, William. I could have refused and then you'd be dead and I'd be alone with my guilt. This was my choice and I don't regret a single decision I've made. That is a promise." She took his lips, kissing the life out of him and showing how certain she was of the decisions she'd taken.

Katie moaned as her body responded to his, instantly coming to life and showing her how much she was attuned to him. She moved the sheet out of the way and looked at him, the glorious length of his cock sticking out to attention. She reached out and touched him. He arched up, crying out in ecstasy. She felt powerful as she held his heat within her palm and knew she could give him either pleasure or pain.

"You're so soft," she moaned as he grasped her hips and he placed her knees to either side of his head. Katie squealed as he penetrated her slit with his tongue. She ground her pussy against his face, instinct taking over. The sensations engulfed her. She looked down at his cock and knew what he wanted, what she wanted to do. She touched him again, feeling the pulsing life within her hand.

A small burst of light shone from the lamp and she got a visual of her head bobbing up and down in his lap. Katie smiled. Her pussy creamed against his face. She grabbed his cock and encircled the tip with her mouth, tasting his salty essence.

"Yes, take me in your mouth," he encouraged her. Katie let the images take over, showing her what he wanted her to do and what he liked. She took him to the back of her throat and tasted him. Coming up to circle the tip with her tongue, then back down. His cock was slippery with her saliva.

"I want inside you," he growled and, using that super vampire speed, he had her on her back and was embedded deep inside her before she had a chance to answer.

She laughed. "I was enjoying tasting you."

"You can taste me any other time but I need to feel you now." And he did.

William shocked her by changing position. He got her on her knees at the edge of the bed. "I'm going to show you everything." He pressed his cock against her cunt from behind, the position wicked and exciting. When the tip stayed inside her, her grabbed her hips with his hands and, with more force than she was prepared for, he thrust inside her. She moaned and William growled. He dug his fingers into the flesh of her hips. She liked the way he was using her body, going as deep as he could, making her writhe from the sensation. It felt dirty and sexy and she loved it. He took them both to new heights neither had ever known existed.

They collapsed in a heap.

"Wouldn't that be cool if we just made a baby," Katie whispered into his ear. He groaned as he ground his hips against her. His cock already growing again at the thought of her being full and pregnant with his child.

"I'm keeping you forever," he told her.

"You promise?" she asked.

"You are my life."

They kissed, happy, at least in this moment where they were together and whole, perhaps with a new life starting within her body.

A precious piece of life — an extension of their love.

William

Epilogue

"What shall we do, sir?"

James looked at his minion, the lowlife not fit to be part of his new order. "I want those fucking Valentines destroyed and I want it doing now."

The rest of the pack remained silent, waiting for him to give them their orders. He winced as the blood continued to trickle from his neck, refusing to congeal. He was dying, unless he could find the cure for a fucking pure-blood vampire bite.

The dirty vermin. They all needed to be destroyed.

"They're searching for the original alpha, sir," one of the human minions said from the floor.

James turned on her. "How do you know this?" he demanded.

The minion twisted her fingers together.

"I work as their cleaner. I'm seen and not heard, sir."

James laughed, laughed and kept on laughing.

"Well, it looks like we have our entrance. I want those Valentines at my feet and then they'll rue the day they questioned me." James thought of the satisfaction he would feel to see all of the vampires killed. Annihilated.

Once he held the key, he would hold all the power, and he would use it. No one would defy him.

"Orders, sir?"

"Release Lewis to me."

"Yes, sir."

The minion scampered off. Lewis — the first and last son of the original alpha. Too bad the kid thought James was his father, and he was about to use him to his full potential.

James wanted the power so much that he would use anything at his disposal and he would use it as he saw fit.

"I'm here, father," Lewis said as he came into the room. James could see the aura of power that surrounded him. The true Alpha was staring right at him. He growled and snapped.

It was time to remove the Valentine women from the equation.

James smiled viciously.

About the Author

Sam Crescent has always had a love of fiction, through her teen years she would find friendship between the pages rather than in an actual person. By the time she turned sixteen she discovered mills and boon and never looked back. She loved the quick happily-ever-after read. A guarantee that no matter what happened the heroes and heroines would always find their soul mate. After college and starting a degree, one lonely bored night she searched the internet looking for a new author to read. On that night and for the years to come she discovered romantica and erotic writing.

Sam Crescent loves to hear from readers. You can find her contact information, website details and author profile page at http://www.total-e-bound.com

Total-E-Bound Publishing

www.total-e-bound.com

Take a look at our exciting range of literagasmic™
erotic romance titles and discover pure quality
at Total-E-Bound.

www.ingramcontent.com/pod-product-compliance
Lightning Source LLC
Chambersburg PA
CBHW021520240626
47154CB00002B/720